WE HAVE THIS HOPE

Sherry M Hefner

"The Homespun Wife"

Table of Contents

CHAPTER ONE 1
    THE UNEXPECTED 1

CHAPTER TWO: 3
    THE INCIDENT 3

CHAPTER THREE: 5
    QUEEN ANNE'S LACE 5

CHAPTER FOUR: 7
    THE DIAGNOSIS 7

CHAPTER FIVE: 9
    EVERLASTING ARMS 9

CHAPTER SIX: 12
    SHOW US THE WAY 12

CHAPTER SEVEN: 15
    THIS OL' WORLD, IT AIN'T MY HOME 15

CHAPTER EIGHT: 19
    LANDON'S FEATHERS 19

CHAPTER NINE: 24
    RECOLLECTIONS 24

CHAPTER TEN: 29
    SAMUEL'S HOMEGOING 29

CHAPTER ELEVEN: 34
    KIN 34

CHAPTER TWELVE: 38
   TROUBLE AT THE MILL 38

CHAPTER THIRTEEN: 41
   MIRIAM FINDS HER COURAGE 41

CHAPTER FOURTEEN: 45
   LANDON'S REQUESTS.. 45

CHAPTER FIFTEEN: 49
   THE OPEN DOOR 49

CHAPTER SIXTEEN: 53
   ABIGAIL'S ANSWERED PRAYER................................... 53

CHAPTER SEVENTEEN: 56
   MIRIAM'S HAPPY DREAM 56

CHAPTER EIGHTEEN: 60
   GRANDMA'S IMPORTANT TRUTHS 60

CHAPTER NINETEEN: 66
   GOD IS LOVE 66

CHAPTER TWENTY: 70
   HEAVEN AND NATURE SING PART ONE 70

CHAPTER TWENTY-ONE: 75
   HEAVEN AND NATURE SING PART TWO 75

CHAPTER TWENTY-TWO: 78
   HEAVEN AND NATURE SING LANDON'S ADDENDUM .. 78

CHAPTER TWENTY-THREE: 82
   TIME TURNS.. 82

CHAPTER TWENTY-FOUR: 85
   WHEN GOD MAKES A FAMILY 85

CHAPTER TWENTY-FIVE: 90
   BEST NURSE EVER.. 90

CHAPTER TWENTY-SIX: 94

THE CALL 94
CHAPTER TWENTY-SEVEN: 99
THE ROAD 99

CHAPTER ONE

THE UNEXPECTED

She was thankful, even though the work was hard and the heat of the day caused sweat to form on her brow. She was thankful for the tomatoes and corn and cucumber that continued to come in. As Miriam toiled, her mind took notice of the filled jars that lined her shelves. She took comfort in knowing that, whatever may come, there would be plenty for them to eat this winter.

While she worked, she hummed an old hymn. Sometimes the words would flow out, like an opened box in her memory. 'Summer and winter and springtime and harvest....,' she sang. As she sang, she heard that distinct popping noise, letting her know the lids had sealed. Miriam smiled with satisfaction. As she removed more hot jars from the oven, she continued her tune, "Great is thy faithfulness, Lord, unto me." She paused momentarily. Yes. God had been faithful.

Miriam wiped her hands on her apron and pushed down the fears she held inside. She glanced out the window, wondering if she would still be around to see these fields next summer. But there was too much that needed doing to stop and worry just now. She reminded herself that God had always taken care of her, even during her troubled childhood, and he wasn't about to stop now. She did her best to shift her focus back to the task at hand, but as she placed the next batch of tomatoes in the canner, Miriam felt her eyes fill with hot tears.

Just then, Landon rounded the corner, breathless and stammering. 'Come quick, Mama. Hurry, it's bad,' he said, as she threw down the towel and went running into the field behind him.

CHAPTER TWO:

THE INCIDENT

Miriam ran with all her might and as she cleared the ridge she saw the blue workhorse tractor as it sat near the apple orchard. Her heart was pounding so fast, not only from the run, but from the anxiety and fear of the unexpected. Soon she spotted Samuel, laid out under the tree. He made no movement and even as she approached and called out his name, he made no sound. His leg was twisted back at an awful angle and she knew without a doubt it was broken. His head was bleeding, too, and she was scared to move him.

Turning to Landon, she said, 'Go at once and get on your bicycle and ride over to Ms. Martha's. Tell her your daddy has fallen from the ladder and we need help quick.' Landon was gone before the last of her sentence was completed and the gravity of the moment came crashing in. She untied her apron and placed it under Samuel's head, very gently, as she began to pray. 'God please help us. Please help us,' she cried out.

It seemed like hours but it was only minutes before John came in a rush, driving his old truck over the fields in a fury. In the front with John was one of his workmen, Phillip, and before Miriam knew it, they had gathered Samuel up on a makeshift pallet in the bed of the truck. As they moved him, Samuel came to and started mumbling and groaning in pain. 'I'm here, Sam...I'm here,' Miriam said. 'Everything will be alright.' But even as she said the words, she wasn't sure of them.

WE HAVE THIS HOPE

As John flew down the two-lane backroad towards town, Miriam sat in the bed of the truck with Samuel, stroking his forehead. His eyes were closed and his breathing was labored. In her heart she prayed, 'Dear Lord, please don't take Sam. Please don't take Sam. He's the only man that's ever been good to me. Lord, you can take everything else we have...but please, not Sam.'

CHAPTER THREE:

QUEEN ANNE'S LACE

As Miriam sat in the waiting room of the hospital, she found herself twisting the strings of the dirty apron in her lap. To tell the truth, everything inside her felt twisted in an awful sort of way. But she knew she had to be strong for Landon. Soon, Ms. Martha and her sister Carrie arrived to offer support. After staying awhile, Ms. Martha suggested that she and Carrie take Landon back home with them, where he could get washed up and have a hot evening meal. She assured Miriam that Landon would be well cared for and that she would see to it that he said his prayers and was safely tucked in at a reasonable hour. Miriam had lost all track of time since then but could see out the window that night had fallen. And still there was no word from the operating room.

Occasionally John would say, "Let's not set to worryin' yet. Doctors can take a whole heap of time gettin' stuff stitched up just right." Philip simply sat with hat in hand, staring at the floor.

As Miriam waited, she recalled the dream she had the night before. In the dream she was standing in the field, across the way from the old barn of her childhood. She hated that old barn and didn't want to think of it and the awful things that had happened there. But as she looked more closely, Miriam noticed that all around her was a thick boundary of Queen Anne's Lace. She loved Queen Anne's Lace, and even though she didn't recall seeing any of it growing around the old barn, there it was in her dream. Miriam recalled it was Sam, on their wedding day, that had explained to her that the Queen Anne's Lace in her simple bouquet symbolized safety and refuge.

As she was thinking on this, the surgeon appeared in the doorway and Miriam stood up when she saw him. "Mrs. Barker, your husband is resting comfortably. I did what I could to repair his leg but I'm just not sure it was enough. It was a critical compound fracture and it's possible he will need more surgery. We have to be watchful for any sign of infection. In addition, when Mr. Barker fell, he hit his head and suffered a skull fracture and concussion." Miriam listened the best she could while trembling all over.

"But Mrs. Barker, there is something much more serious I need to discuss with you. My nurse will be out shortly to show you to my office."

Miriam's heart sank. In that moment, she longed to be with Sam in a field of Queen Anne's Lace. More than anything, she just wanted them to be together and safe."

CHAPTER FOUR:

THE DIAGNOSIS

The anticipation was almost more than Miriam could bear and she was relieved when the doctor finally entered the office where she had been waiting. She noticed he held a file of papers in his hand as he pulled his chair to the desk.

'Mrs. Barker, tell me. Has your husband been having any health problems lately?,' he asked.

'Well, yes he has,' Miriam answered, 'but we assumed he was just tired is all. We've been under a strain, trying to keep the farm work up, you know. It's just the three of us, me and Sam and our young son, Landon. And we've been trying to harvest more this summer with things being as hard as they are all over. Sam's been extra tired and having headaches but he doesn't believe in complaining much. And he's also been sweating pretty bad overnight and that's something he's never done before.'

The doctor wrote down a few notes and then spoke. 'Mrs. Barker, your husband is very sick. It's my opinion he fell off the ladder because his strength and balance are being compromised by his cancer.'

Miriam was stunned. 'Cancer?'

'Yes, ma'am. I'm very sorry to bring you this news. At this stage, I can't be sure where the cancer originated but it appears to be widespread. Unfortunately, we have no treatment for it, Mrs. Barker. There is nothing we can do. I know this comes as a shock to you. But for now, we will keep Mr. Barker here in the hospital and assist him the best we can.'

Miriam felt sick and unsure of what to say next. But she had to say something. 'Does..does he know, doctor? Does Sam know what's happening?'

The doctor shook his head. 'Not yet because he's still not awake from the surgery. But as soon as it's possible, I will give him a full update. My advice to you is to let your friends take you home, Mrs. Barker. There isn't anything you can do here tonight. It's been a long day, and you need rest. Go on home and try to sleep. If anything changes in the overnight hours, we can call you.'

'We don't have a phone out at our place. But our neighbors do. Our neighbors are John and Martha Long and he's the one out there waiting with me. His wife is watching over our son at their farmhouse,' Miriam responded.

'Perhaps you could join your son then and stay the night with your neighbors so we will have a way to reach you, if needed.' The doctor handed her a slip of paper and a pencil so she could write down the Long's number. And with that, the doctor abruptly stood up from behind his desk and left his office.

The air in the room was stifling and Miriam could hardly breathe. Her mind couldn't process what she had just been told. She was too numb to cry, even though everything inside felt like it was coming apart.

In her mind, she was trying to come to terms with this new reality: Sam had cancer and there was nothing they could do.

CHAPTER FIVE:

EVERLASTING ARMS

Miriam rose early, while it was still dark outside. She hadn't slept well and had too much on her mind to linger in bed. As she moved about the room, she was careful not to waken Landon, who was sleeping comfortably. How would she tell Landon that his daddy was very sick with a terminal illness? How would the two of them ever survive on their own? How could she go on living without Sam?

She combed her long hair and braided it, wrapping the braid like a crown around her head. Sam liked it that way. She was thankful John had taken the extra time last night to run her up to the house so she could gather a few things. She hated to impose on Ms. Martha, asking her to watch over Landon temporarily for the next few days. But truth was, Miriam had no one else.

As she stepped out into the hallway, she saw the light of the kitchen was already on. She smelled coffee and biscuits and heard a soft humming sound. Miriam rounded the corner to see Ms. Martha, apron tied and fork in hand, starting to fry up some bacon in the cast iron skillet.

Ms. Martha turned as she realized Miriam had entered the kitchen, and she promptly walked over and embraced Miriam in the warmest hug. Miriam bristled at first, but soon felt her heart give way as she began to cry. As her tears flowed, Ms. Martha spoke gently, "It's going to be alright dear. God is in control."

Miriam withdrew at those words. She didn't want to hear them. She spoke abruptly, "If he's in control, why is he letting this happen to Sam? Why is he doing this to us...to me?!"

Ms. Martha wasn't caught off guard by Miriam's questions or her doubts. "Sweet child," she said. "Sometimes things just happen. It's one of life's great mysteries. Bad things happen to good people. Good things happen to bad people. We don't have all the answers. But what the good Lord wants us to do is learn to trust him with everything. He's the only hope we have, Miriam. And when hard times come, and they come to everyone sooner or later, we have to lean on his everlasting arms. Now let's get you something to eat so you can get to the hospital this morning. Your man will be expecting you."

And with that, Ms. Martha returned to cooking. As she worked she sang in soft tones, "What have I to dread, what have I to fear, Leaning on the everlasting arms. I have blessed peace with my Lord so near, Leaning on the everlasting arms..."

Miriam had heard the old hymn in church before but had never really paid attention to the lyrics. As she heard them, she thought to herself, "But, Lord, I do have dread and tons of fear. Are you really here? Do you even care?"

About that time, John appeared in the kitchen, looking weary and a bit older than yesterday. He told Miriam he would drive her to the hospital as soon as they had breakfast. While Ms. Martha set the table, Miriam went back down the hall to dress Landon for the day. She explained to him that daddy had come through surgery and he would need time to get over it. Miriam knew there was no need to tell him anything more at this point. Instead, she promised Landon she would take him to visit daddy as soon as the doctor said it was allowed.

Over breakfast, John said the blessing and prayed that God would be with Sam and give him healing. He also prayed for Miriam, that God would give her strength and peace, and that God would also give Landon a good day with Ms. Martha.

Before long, the table was cleared and Miriam was anxious to get to the hospital. She hugged little Landon and was soon riding down the winding road, towards town. Miriam noticed that late summer was giving way to early fall colors. She thought back to the many dreams she had with Sam and realized those dreams would likely never happen.

Miriam had no idea what she would face at the hospital. She wondered what Sam might say or what he would be feeling once he got the news. She hoped she could comfort him or say the right things but she was probably too upset for that. Miriam had never been a warm or affectionate person. She didn't know how. Her mama had been sick during her whole childhood and her father, cold and distant, was rarely home. After the experience in the barn, Miriam was even more removed. Now, at just 25 years old, she was starting to assume that she was more like her father than she cared to admit.

As the truck made its way across the countryside, Miriam closed her eyes to the early morning sun and unexpectedly found herself imagining what it might be like to lean on Jesus' everlasting arms. In that moment, her mind and heart felt so much peace that she slipped into a much needed sleep for the rest of the trip.

CHAPTER SIX:

SHOW US THE WAY

As Miriam made her way down the long hospital hallway, she reached up to make sure her hair was still properly tucked in place. She was apprehensive, even as she tried to calm herself. She found Sam's room and tapped lightly on his door before turning the knob to enter.

The first sight of him broke her heart. She had tried to prepare herself for how Sam might appear just one day after his terrible fall and the long surgery that followed, but she was still surprised. Pale and obviously in pain, he tried to reach out to her. Miriam did her best not to be emotional as she drew to his bedside and took his hand. She leaned down to kiss his forehead but couldn't contain the tears that were slipping out.

"Miriam...Miriam," Sam whispered. "It will be ok."

She wanted to argue with him and set him straight. It wasn't going to be ok. He was dying and nothing could be done about it. But she felt it wasn't appropriate to fuss about it now, as he was just coming to terms with things for himself.

"Sit, darlin'," he said, and she did. She slid the straight back chair close to his bedside and looked down into Sam's eyes.

"Did the doctor come by this morning?," she asked.

"He did," Sam answered. "It wasn't the news we was expectin' but I knew I wasn't doing well, Miriam. Something was wrong. And deep inside, you knew it too. The most important thing we can do now is get you and Landon ready to go forward from here. You have to, Miriam. I know you'll be grievin' but we gotta make a plan for you."

Miriam wasn't ready to have this kind of talk. She desperately wanted to run down the hall and out the hospital doors. And she would have run if she had somewhere to go. But she didn't. Sam was her everything. Sam and Landon. How could she possibly plan for a life without Sam?

As she shook her head no, Sam continued talking softly. "They're gonna come here in a minute with my pain medicine but I asked 'em to hold off so I could be clearheaded to talk to ya, Miriam. We gotta make a plan. But the first thing we gotta do is pray about it. There's no use in plans if we don't ask God what to do. He's gonna show us, Miriam, so don't be worryin'."

"Sam, aren't you scared? Aren't you fighting with God about how he's let you get sick like this? This isn't right. You're a good man. You're hardworking and kind. You go to church and pray. We've got a child to raise and farm to tend and times are already so hard and...." Miriam's voice cracked as she could speak no more words.

"Listen here, darlin'. There's no need a blamin' God. Sure, I'm not happy about this. No man wants to face this kind of fate. But God knows what he's doin'. Who am I to question it? He knows what's best and if this is what's best, then I have to go along with it. And so do you."

"I do not! I will not!" Miriam yelled out, before clasping her hand over her mouth, as if to stifle her defiance.

"Miriam. Steady yourself." Sam winced in pain. "We're gonna stop and pray now and God will help us."

Miriam lowered her head, as Sam slid his hand into her lap. His own voice was breaking as he started, "Dear Lord. We're troubled. We wasn't expectin' this bad news. But we're puttin' our trust in you, even if it's hard. And Lord, we need help. We need a plan for Miriam and Landon. And we'll do what you say. Lord, heaven's my home and even though I'd like to stay right here, I'm not afraid to go. But I'm worried for my family. We need to know what to do next. We got all our hope in you, so show us the way. Lord, Show us the way. In Jesus' name, Amen."

Sam squeezed Miriam's hand. She could sense his strength was greatly diminished. And then he said something she wasn't at all ready to hear: "I know one thing for sure, Miriam. One day, when the time is right, you're gonna need to tell Landon the truth. You can tell him I loved him and considered him my own. But he deserves to know I'm not his father."

CHAPTER SEVEN:

THIS OL' WORLD, IT AIN'T MY HOME

In the few days following Miriam's hospital talk with Sam, she set about doing all the things they had discussed were best. She had taken Landon and gone out to the house, where she gathered the items she would keep. To one corner, she set aside the things that would be sold, and that included her canner and canning jars. She would have no place for them in the immediate days ahead.

At moments her resolve would break, and she would sit on the edge of the bed to cry. She didn't want to doubt God or his care for them, but she still questioned how he could let good people suffer. Miriam could hear Landon outside, as he rolled his wagon from the back of the house. Sam had told her, early that morning on her daily visit, "Bring him to me, Miriam, and I will tell him about the cancer." She dreaded that. She didn't know how she would ever comfort Landon once he learned his daddy was dying.

Sam, for his part, was holding up well despite the fact his leg was causing him quite a bit of pain and the doctor had indicated he didn't think Sam would get to go home before things became, "critical." Sam took the news as best as he could, even though his eyes welled with tears at the thought he would never see the farm again.

Just as Miriam was feeling overwhelmed, she heard Landon's laughter, followed by singing. As she stepped into the kitchen, she saw Ms. Martha and Carrie, carrying a cloth sack and coming up the path. As Miriam opened the door, Ms. Martha smiled, "Good Morning dearie! We've come to help. We brought our cleaning supplies and two strong backs....well, as strong as two old women can offer!" And with that Ms. Martha laughed heartily. And even though Carrie was the quiet, stoic sister, she smiled sweetly at Ms. Martha's amusement. "Now don't you worry, Miriam. We will have this place sorted in no time at all. And then you and Landon can move down to our farm full-time. It's going to be so good to have a young fella around the place again...and to have you, too. Always wanted a girl, we did. But God didn't find it to be in his plan, which is quite alright. He knows best." And with that, she and Carrie set in to sweeping, wiping, and organizing.

For lunch, Ms. Martha had packed leftover chicken, potato salad, pickles, and what remained of the morning's biscuits. Landon ate a full plate and Miriam noted how quickly he was growing. Monday would find Landon starting second grade and John had seen to it that Landon had a new pair of shoes and dungarees. Even Carrie had gone to the general store and bought Landon two nice shirts for the new school year. Miriam would be forever grateful for how this family had taken them in.

As they worked during the early afternoon, Ms. Martha sang old songs she had learned long ago. Miriam had never seen a working woman look so happy and fulfilled while doing her chores.

"Well, this ol' world, it ain't my home,

it ain't my home, it ain't my home.

No this ol' world, it ain't my home

My home's in Glory Land..."

she belted out in her alto voice.

"One day soon, I'm goin' by,

I'm goin' by, I'm goin' by.

Yes one day soon I'm goin' by

To my home in Glory Land."

By midafternoon, most everything was done that needed doing. Aside from the few boxes Miriam would keep, everything else would be sold at auction and the bank would be taking back the farm.

"Little lad," Ms. Martha said, "gather your things and walk back with me and Aunt Carrie. Let your mama finish her doings. I need you to gather me up some sticks so I can be cooking some cornbread for supper. I'm thinking of making up a pie. What say you, Landon? What do you think of an apple pie?"

"Yes ma'am! I like that idea a bunch! Will Mr. Long let me try peeling them apples with his little knife, Ms. Martha? Will he, will he? I'll be real careful and I'll sit still, I promise."

"Well we'll see about that, little lad. You're right young to be usin' a pocket knife."

"I'm starting second grade on Monday, Ms. Martha. I'm growed up!," responded Landon, arguing his case. That statement caused Carrie to chuckle audibly, as they went down the dirt path toward the Long's farm.

Miriam looked around the little place that she and Sam had called home. This was the home where they had brought baby Landon after he was first born. It's where Sam had coaxed him into taking his first steps. It was there, at the table, where Miriam had held her breath as Sam had a taste of her first lemon pound cake. She could still see the smile he gave her, signaling his full approval. In that corner to the left, they had put up their Christmas tree each year. It was full of paper ornaments and dried fruits and small bits of fabric stitchings.

And now, those days were done.

As Miriam closed the door to leave, she paused to take one last look at the farm. She had no tears left to cry. She simply stood and took it all in. And in that moment, she heard Ms. Martha's song playing like a recording in her heart...

"No this ol' world it ain't my home,

My home's in Glory Land...."

CHAPTER EIGHT:

LANDON'S FEATHERS

The day Miriam had dreaded finally arrived. It was time to take Landon to visit his daddy. Landon was excited for the day and couldn't wait to give his dad a hug. Miriam had finished making up their bed and walked to the kitchen to see if Landon was ready to go.

"He's outside with the chickens, Miriam," Ms. Martha said. "I couldn't say no to him. He told me he needed to go out there to get something to take his daddy this morning."

Miriam glanced out the side window to see Landon in the chicken run, gathering feathers. She went to the door and called out, "Don't be getting dirty, Landon. We're about to go to town. Come and get washed up. Daddy is waiting."

It didn't take long for Landon to run inside, clutching his feathers, and talking a mile a minute. Miriam combed his hair for the third time that morning and washed the breakfast remnants from his face.

The drive to the hospital was entertaining, as Landon talked about school and a new friend he had made. "He ain't from here, mama. He's from Kentucky and his daddy came down here to get some work. And his clothes are sorta tore right here, where the buttons go. But it don't matter, does it, mama? I told him, 'Don't worry 'bout that, Kenny, cause it don't matter. I got tored up shirts, too.'"

As they approached Sam's room, Miriam bent down to remind Landon that his daddy was very sick. "His leg is still hurting so you can't jump on him or wrestle, ok? We have to be on our best behavior." To this news, Landon shook his head in agreement.

As Miriam pushed opened the door, she noticed right away that Sam wasn't looking very good. He had gone down since yesterday and that fact welled up in her and filled her with momentary panic. But she was glad the panic passed quickly.

Sam opened his eyes and his face lit up when he saw his boy, standing there near his bed. "Landon! You've come to see me! Don't be scared now. It's alright. Come over and take my hand." And Landon did. "I sure have missed you. But mama says you're liking school."

"I am, daddy. I got a new friend and his name is Kenny. And he's from Kentucky. And he's real nice and he likes to go fishing and we're gonna go one day. And he ain't scared of worms or nothin' and he can bait hooks. And I can, too. I can bait hooks just like you taught me, daddy."

"Why, you're the best at baitin' hooks of anybody I ever saw, Landon. And I know you'll be catchin' some mighty fine fish soon enough. I'm awful proud of the good fella you are. You take good care of mama and you go to school and study. You bait hooks and go to church. You're an example for other boys to follow." With Sam's kind words, Landon stood ten foot tall.

He continued, "But there's somethin' we got talk about, son. So I need you to sit up in this chair. I know you're just a young boy and all. But I gotta talk to you like a man today. So I hope you'll listen good, like a man would."

"I will, daddy. I can listen good," Landon said sincerely.

"Landon, I'm real sick and the truth is, I'm not gonna be gettin' better. What I got, they can't fix it. So I'm gonna be goin' to heaven to see Jesus soon. And I know it's sad for me and you and your mama, too. It's not easy to talk about. But I gotta say it straight, Landon. You're gonna be the man of the house. And I'm gonna need you to be strong.

I'm expectin' you to obey your mama even when it's hard. And I want you to keep goin' to school. Get all the schoolin' you can because that's important to gettin' yourself a good job in life. And I want you to keep on bein' kind to everyone."

"But daddy," Landon interjected, "ain't you comin' home? Ain't hospitals s'pposed to get sick folks well and all?"

Sam responded, "Hospitals try hard to get sick folks well, Landon, you're right. But sometimes people got sicknesses that hospitals can't fix. And sometimes, even though we pray and ask God for healin', his plan is to take people to heaven instead. And there's no use in bein' mad at God over it. Cause God's got a plan. I can't see it. You can't see. Not yet. But God's got a plan and his plan is to take me to heaven and for you and mama to stay here on earth doin' the things he's gonna show you to do. So never stop prayin' and listenin' to God, Landon. Never stop lovin' God. Cause he sure does love you."

Landon, with eyes cast down in his lap, was finally silent. Miriam was in the corner, crying quietly, and wondering how she would ever recover from what she was witnessing that day.

"Landon," Sam continued, "it's ok to be sad or cry. Everybody feels like that sometimes. But there comes a time when we gotta let the sadness go and we gotta move on to the next thing that needs doin'. Cause life is for the livin'. Don't forget that. Life is for the livin' and as long as God's got you here on earth, he's got things for you to do. You're gonna grow up and get yourself a fam'ly of your own one day. And they'll need you."

"But daddy. Our family needs you, too." Landon's voice was so soft that Miriam could hardly hear it.

"I know, son. But God's got other plans for me. And I know it's hard to accept it but we got to. We gotta trust God. God's gonna look after you and mama. And I just want you to know that no matter what happens....I love you. You're my son and I'm very proud of you. For a long time I prayed for a child and God gave me you. And I'm so very grateful for that. So grateful." Sam's voice cracked and Miriam could see his tears falling to the pillow.

Miriam stepped out of the shadows just then and placed her hand on Landon's shoulder. "I think daddy's getting tired, son. We should let him rest and maybe we can come back soon to see him again."

"Can I ask something else, daddy?"

"Sure, Landon," Sam answered. "Ask anything you want."

"Daddy, what's heaven like?"

Sam closed his eyes, as if he was seeing it in real time. "Son, it's so beautiful in heaven. There's nothing on earth so nice as heaven cause God's designed it just for us, with pearly gates and streets of gold. He's got us a perfect place to live and it won't never need fixin' up. And we won't get sick up there and we won't hurt or cry no more. And all the people we read about in the Bible? They're there! Why, there's Moses and King David and the Apostle Paul. Not only that but my mama is there. You never got to meet her but she

sure woulda loved to seen you. Yes she would. I'm looking forward to seein' mama and daddy again. But most important, Jesus is there! I can't wait to see him best of all. It's gonna be worth everythin' we have to go through on this ol' earth just to see his face. And we get to be with Jesus forever and ever once we get to heaven. Ain't that something wonderful, son? And there's gonna be singing and praising and they's gonna be lots of angels flying all around, with wings of white." As Sam talked, he began to drift. It was evident he was exhausted.

"Ok, Landon. That's enough for now. Let's tell daddy bye and we will see him later."

Miriam took Landon by the hand as she prepared to leave.

But Landon turned back, quickly returning to his daddy's bed.

He whispered quietly, as Sam slept, and carefully reached up to hold his dad's hand. "I listened like a man, daddy, just like you said for me to. So don't worry 'bout nothin'. I'll be strong and take care of mama and get schoolin' and love God, just like you said. And I got you somethin', daddy. I got you some feathers. You can keep 'em and show 'em to the angels. You can tell them angels that you got feathers, too. And... And... I love you, daddy."

CHAPTER NINE:

RECOLLECTIONS

As the days drew closer for Sam's departure, Miriam was surprised to find an internal peace she couldn't explain. Even though she often felt sad, she tried to allow the grief to pass, just as Sam had instructed. Sam had said that grief was acceptable for a time but she shouldn't become overwhelmed by it. Instead, she should decide to let go of the sadness and focus on the things that needed doing.

Sam's words of guidance were such a comfort for her now, especially since Sam was no longer able to speak. It was a good thing that, the previous week, he had completed all the conversations he needed to have. In one of his last talks, he had spoken plainly to John, thanking him and Ms. Martha for allowing Miriam and Landon to live on their farm and for providing food, shelter, and emotional support. But Sam told John that once his death occurred, Miriam would be taking Landon and going into town to work at the textile mill. She would rent a room there in the mill village. John had responded by insisting that Miriam and Landon stay with them, at least until the Christmas season had passed. But Sam had grown tired by that point and drifted to sleep. The plans were never mentioned again.

In recalling these things, Miriam felt the urge to go for a walk. She was feeling restless and needed fresh air to sort out her thoughts. She dreaded life without Sam. She dreaded returning to the mill. It was Sam, after all, who had rescued her from the terrible situation in which she had found herself. Thinking back, Miriam remembered how alone she had felt the day her mother died. Her mother had been bedridden for so long that Miriam could never recall a day when her mother felt well enough to sit at the table for a meal or to take a walk outside in the sunshine. Even so, she had been a constant presence in Miriam's life, unlike her father. He had been mostly absent, not only from their home, but from their lives. The community around them had tried to take turns looking after them, coming to bring food sometimes. But after her mother's death, Miriam had no reason to stay. After fleeing from home late one night, she walked through the darkness for miles until she reached town, where she collapsed on the steps of the Ora Textile Mill.

It was there, while working in the spinning room, that Miriam first saw Sam. She learned that Sam was a sharecropper who had just purchased a small abandoned farm but still worked as hired help for anyone who required hard labor. On the day he first spoke to Miriam, Sam was delivering cotton to the mill and she was outside taking a quick break from the lint and noise. As he passed by, he introduced himself as Sam and said, "I can tell you're a hard worker. Every time I'm here you're up on your feet, givin' it your all. Why, I ain't never seen you take no breaks." She didn't say anything but tried to smile without making eye contact. He continued, "I been told you're Miriam. So it's nice to meet you Miriam." Once again, she smiled but looked away.

Over the next few weeks, Miriam saw Sam several times and he was always nice to her and tried to make conversation. But she knew she needed to avoid him. She was no good for anyone and after all that had happened, she was certain no one would ever want her.

Late one afternoon as she was leaving her shift, Miriam had stepped outside and immediately felt faint. She had been sick quite a bit and she knew why but no one else did. At that very moment, Sam appeared and knelt down to help her up. He took her to his truck and gave her some water. She began crying and heaving all at once. Sam did his best to calm her but she was both sick and inconsolable. Suddenly, there was a clap of thunder and the rains began to pour.

"You gotta get all the way up in the truck now, ma'am," Sam said, "or you're gonna get soaked." She pulled her legs inside and leaned her head back against the glass window. She closed her eyes but Sam kept talking, "Whatever is goin' on, Miriam, it ain't the end of the world. I know you're mighty upset 'bout somethin' but God's gonna work things out. That's what God does best, you know. He works things out."

"He can't work things out for me. He can't...no one can," Miriam said. Her voice was soft and resolute. She was giving up.

"Miriam. don't say that now. God's powerful. He's lookin' after you, even if you don't know it," Sam said.

"If God was looking after me, he wouldn't have let my mama die. He wouldn't have let...," Miriam's voice trailed off.

There was silence for a moment and she was terribly uncomfortable with it. Suddenly she blurted out the truth. "I'm with child, Sam. I'm with child and there's...there's...there's no father. I mean, there is one but...he's....a terrible person," she sobbed.

"Miriam. Listen here. It's gonna be alright. There's no need to despair. Even when things are bad, there's hope." Sam said.

"I know how people are! I know. They will judge me. And you will too! You are judging me even now," she grimaced.

"No ma'am. I ain't judgin' you. I got no place to judge nobody. I just know you're a nice lady. You work hard. And I want to help you any way I can."

It was in the following moments that Sam hatched a remarkable plan. He suggested that Miriam marry him. It would mostly be a marriage in name only. But no one would question anything when her baby was born. He said, "I just bought an old place. I ain't got much. But together, with hard work, I believe we could do alright. We could help each other out. And we could raise the child out on the farm. And nobody would know nothin' bout nothin', 'cept you and me."

Miriam was in disbelief at first. How could any man want to do something like that? But Sam did. He made it clear he expected nothing of her in the marriage agreement except that they would work together and make a good life. And that's what they did.

One night, before Landon was born, Miriam had cried and cried. She broke down and told Sam about what happened in the barn. She told him how, the day after they buried her mother, she was out in the barn trying to find anything of value that might be sold. She had no money and hadn't seen her father in months. She wasn't sure what to do next.

"And that's when it happened, Sam. That's when daddy's runabout friend appeared out of nowhere in the barn. He...He...attacked me, Sam. He hit me and I screamed and screamed but no one was around to hear. And he did things. And to this day I hate barns. Please don't ever ask me to go in the barn. Please, Sam," she cried. Sam had reached out and held her close, quieting her anxiety.

Little by little, in learning to trust and to confide and to cling together, love grew between Sam and Miriam. And it grew strong and fierce.

Suddenly, Miriam came to and realized she had been lost in her thoughts for a long time. Seeing that the sun was sinking lower, she figured It was nearing supper time now. But as she turned to go, Miriam paused and glanced back for one last look at the beautiful sunset. In was then the Spirit spoke to her heart and revealed something important to her.

"Dear Heavenly Father," she prayed, "Thank you for Sam. What a good husband he has always been to me. Thank you for bringing him into my life. I love him so much. Please reward him for all the good he has done. And forgive me. Forgive me when I've doubted you.

Truth is, I'm scared but I finally get it. Sam came to my rescue. But, Lord, you're the one who saved me. You saved me. And somehow you'r gonna keep working things out because working things out is what you do best."

CHAPTER TEN:

SAMUEL'S HOMEGOING

On the morning Jesus called Samuel home, Miriam held his hand as he crossed into glory. The night before, she had decided to stay at the hospital because she felt his time was near. She had washed his face with a warm cloth and combed his hair, which had grown longer with each passing day. She was pleased that, while his breathing had grown shallow, he appeared comfortable and at peace.

Miriam talked to Sam all through the night, recalling fun memories, such as the time she jumped up on the kitchen chair, squealing with fear, as Sam chased a field mouse out of the house with a broom. There was also the time early in their marriage she tried to hem a pair of second-hand church pants but ended up making the right side shorter than the left. The mistake wasn't discovered until Sam had dressed for church the following Sunday morning and Miriam was horrified. Sam decided to wear them anyway, despite Miriam's protests. "Miriam, darlin'," he had said, "You never had nobody teachin' you sewin' and such when you was growin' up, so you're still figuring' it out. I think you done very good for your first try and I'm proud of you. So I'm wearin' 'em." And that was the end of that.

As the night wore on, Miriam read aloud from the Psalms, and also from Hebrews 11 and 12, which were some of Sam's favorite passages. "...Let us lay aside every weight, and the sin which doth so easily beset us, and let us run with patience the race that is set before us..."

At points, she would rest her head on the edge of Sam's bed and sleep, waking up periodically to check on him. She would kiss his forehead and touch her fingers to his cheek. She tried not to think that this would be last night she could do these things. As dawn neared, Miriam began to softly sing. She wasn't as gifted as Ms. Martha, but she did the best she could. Somehow, she ended up singing an old lullaby that she used to sing to Landon...

Sleep my child and peace attend thee,

All through the night

Guardian angels God will send thee,

All through the night

Soft the drowsy hours are creeping,

Hill and dale in slumber sleeping

I my loved ones' watch am keeping,

All through the night

It was while singing the lullaby that she felt Sam squeeze her hand for the last time on earth.

As the first light began to break in the sky, Sam started to move. Miriam talked to him, "Sam, what is it?" But he only reached upward and appeared to mouth the word, "Home," although he made no sound. "It's ok, honey," she said reassuringly, "it's ok. Go home. Landon and I will be fine. You've prepared us well. God will make a way, just like you said. Sam....thank you for all you've done for me. You'll never know...never know....," Miriam whispered. "You taught me about love. And I will always love you." In that moment, Sam let out his last breath, and went to be with the Lord.

It was only then that Miriam cried. She wept not only from sadness and exhaustion, but from the closeness she felt to God in that moment. It was an unexpected emotion, like a last gift that she and Sam could share....the closeness of the Spirit as he came to them and took her husband home.

The funeral service was on a Thursday, as the leaves blew around them and sun shone brightly in the azure sky. The little church was filled to capacity and all listened intently while the minister spoke of Sam's Christian witness and his many acts of selfless service. But what was most surprising was when the minister took a paper from his pocket. "When Sam learned of his cancer, he asked me to transcribe this note to read at his service and I want to share that with you now."

'Dear Friends, My words will be short. I just wanted to say life is for the living. Don't take one minute for granted. Don't spend time standing around and grieving. That's a waste. Spend that time doing something nice for others. Be a friend. Serve God out of love. Forgive people because we all mess up. Remember that everything down here is temporary. I'm realizing that now more than ever. I can't even get out of bed to go back to my farm one last time. We can't take nothing with us when we go. So don't get worked up over stuff like land and houses and tractors. That's a waste. Remember to keep your hope in Jesus.

I am grateful for you all. But mostly I am grateful for my sweet Miriam and my son Landon. You know how I love them and I ask your prayers for them. I will see you all again one day. Goodbye."

The sanctuary was completely quiet, except for the wiping of tears. And Miriam had never been so proud of Sam as in that moment. While they made their way out of the church, the congregation sang:

What a fellowship, what a joy divine,

leaning on the everlasting arms;

what a blessedness, what a peace is mine,

leaning on the everlasting arms.

Miriam dreaded going to the cemetery worst of all. It brought back all the memories of her mother's graveside service. She was worried she would feel that same despair but she didn't. Instead she found a strength that was not her own, as she place a single stem of Queen Anne's lace on Sam's casket.

As the car pulled around to take them home, Miriam suddenly realized how weary she was. She felt she could sleep for hours and still not be fully rested.

In the midst of the silence, Landon spoke up and asked, "Mama, is daddy in heaven?"

Miriam answered, "Yes son, he is. You remember daddy talking to you about this, right? Daddy is with Jesus."

Landon said, "Yes, mama, but is daddy resting in Jesus' arms?"

Miriam paused before she responded. She had to smile at Landon's childlike faith. She knew some people might delve into doctrine or theology to explain things about heaven and eternity to Landon. But even she was still learning about those deep matters for herself.

"I suppose you could say that daddy is resting in the arms of Jesus, yes, Landon."

Landon continued, "And we're leanin' on Jesus' everlastin' arms, mama?"

"Yes we are son," Miriam said.

Landon was quiet for a moment and then spoke up, "Well if daddy's restin' in the arms of Jesus and you and me is leanin' on the arms of Jesus, I reckon we's all togetherlike with Jesus. Ain't that right, mama?"

Miriam reached over and wrapped her son close to her side. She knew he was wrestling with be separated from his daddy.

"I reckon so, Landon. I reckon' me and you and daddy are all togetherlike with Jesus," she said.

"I'm staying close to Jesus, mama. Cause daddy's with him. Ain't you staying close to Jesus, mama?"

"Yes I am, son. Yes I am," Miriam affirmed, as she rested her head against the window and closed her eyes to Autumn's dappled light.

CHAPTER ELEVEN:

KIN

The day after Samuel's funeral, Miriam did very little. She slept later than usual and so did Landon. Since it was a Friday, and the week had been so hard for them, Miriam let Landon stay home from school. When Ms. Martha heard them stirring around, she swept in to check on them, bringing a tray of breakfast for them to enjoy in bed.

"I'm sorry we overslept," Miriam said.

"Oh my. Don't you think a thing of it, child. You and Landon need to rest. Now eat up and take a slow day," she said, as she squeezed Miriam's hand, and then turned to leave. Ms. Martha started to sing before she even left the room, "Take time to be holy, let Him be thy Guide." Miriam closed her eyes to take in the words, "And run not before Him, whatever betide. In joy or in sorrow, still follow the Lord, And looking to Jesus, still trust in His Word."

Once she and Landon finished eating, Miriam dressed him warmly and sent him outside. "Go out and find Mr. John or Mr. Phillip," she instructed. "Tell them you are ready to do some chores to help out. Work is a very good habit. Your daddy was a hard worker. He always liked to make himself useful. And now, while you are young, is a good time to learn how to be useful."

"Yes, ma'am, mama. I know about bein' useful and stuff. Cause I'm gettin' growed up. And I can feed the chickens scraps and I can carry wood to the stack and I can sweep the front steps for Ms. Martha and...I'm useful, mama."

Miriam smiled, "You sure are, son. You are very useful. And I'm proud of you."

After lunch, Miriam asked to have a sit-down talk at the kitchen table with John and Ms. Martha. Phillip kept Landon busy while Miriam discussed future plans. "I want to say a sincere thank you for your kindness to my family over these many weeks. It's been a blessing that you took us in. We had nowhere else to go so I'm grateful. You are good, Christian folk, and I could never repay you even if I tried. I want you to know I'm going to do as Sam and I planned. I will go to town next week to take a job with the mill and I will find us a room to rent so you can get back to normal here on the farm."

"No." Miriam could hear the stern nature of John's voice, as he pushed his coffee aside. He leaned forward with elbows on the table and said, "Miriam, truth is, me and mama need you to stay here on the farm. We ain't gettin' no younger and we, well, we'd be mighty pleased if you'd stay here with your boy. He's right at home on the farm, ya know. Boys need farms and farms need boys. Why, Landon likes the chickens and he likes runnin' free and he's learnin' to milk the cow. Right now he's a makin' a scarecrow with Phillip and he's havin' the best ol' time." Miriam was quiet because she felt John wasn't quite finished. "Now iffin you're wantin' to work for some income, I can rightly see that. But Kenneth Reynolds down on Falls Ridge has two girls who work in the mill and he takes 'em right past here early of a mornin' and picks 'em up of an afternoon. He said he wouldn't mind a-gettin' you and drivin' you regular."

Miriam was taking all this under consideration, when John continued, "And truth is, well...truth is....we see you as kin. Me and mama has got attached. We ain't got no grand-youngins or nothin' and well... truth is we really want ya to stay. It ain't no trouble a-tall. Nary a bit." Miriam took note that Mr. John's chin was trembling.

"John and Ms. Martha, these are the kindest words I've just about ever heard. You've already done so much for us. But there are two things I would need to do in order to stay here. One, I would need you to let me partake in some of the housekeeping and let Landon help out doing chores. That's only right in a household. And two, I would need to pay some room and board."

John interrupted, "No ma'am, young lady. Me and mama can't have that. It won't be right. We do ok and live off the land. And I can't be takin' funds from a widow woman that's my kin."

"Thank you for that, John. And thank you, Ms. Martha. I can see you shaking your head in agreement. But I have to contribute something to the household from my income at the mill. Samuel would be awfully disappointed in me for not doing that. I know I won't be making a lot, especially at first. And I know I have some outstanding hospital bills. But let me offer something for our keep. That way, I will feel like a contributing member of this family." Miriam waited and then went on. "It will make me feel like I'm really kin because in a family, everyone gives something for the good of the whole."

John looked down as he rubbed his thumbs. Finally he said, "I will agree to takin' 10% of whatever you earn per month. That will cover a room for you and a separate one for Landon. He's gettin' of an age to need his own space. And that will cover food and incidentals, like school supplies for the boy. And of the 10% you give us, me and mama will tithe to the church."

Miriam looked at these two precious souls and felt tears welling up in her eyes. Miriam not only had a safe place to stay, but she had a family. God had given her stand-in parents. He had given Landon stand-in grandparents, which is something she never had for herself but always wanted. She wouldn't mind working in the mill with the Reynolds girls. She knew of them from church and had noticed they were quiet, but always said a soft, "Good morning," and, "God bless you."

In that moment, Landon came running inside. He went straight to Mr. John. "Mr. John, Mr. John!! I done made a scarecrow! It's got a hat and all. It's got eyes I put on it. Mr. Phillip said scarecrows ain't really s'pposed to have eyes. But I said mine is." Landon began pulling on Mr. John's hand. "Come see it, come see it. We's 'bout to put it up in the cornfield!" Mr. John reached over before he stepped outside and patted Miriam's small hand. "Look what you done, young lady. You made mama happy-cry."

Through her tears, Ms. Martha said, "Don't ever forget, sweet Miriam. God answers prayers. Just when you think he's forgot, he shows you he's been working on it all along." Ms. Martha slid her chair closer to Miriam and drew her into a warm embrace. How comforting it felt to receive motherly love! And somehow, as Miriam held Ms. Martha in her arms, she felt she was giving motherly love at the same time.

"You're right, Ms. Martha," Miriam said. "God has been working on my prayers all along and I didn't even realize it."

"He's been working on mine for many years, sweet Miriam. Matter of fact, now would be a good time to tell you about our son." Miriam was caught off guard. She didn't know anything about the Longs having a child. She just assumed John called Ms. Martha, "mama," as an endearment. After all, she had been a mother figure to many women in their community. Ms. Martha wiped a tear with the hem of her apron but soon grew resolute. "John and I had a son," she pronounced, "and he was our pride and joy. He was all we had. But he's gone now and we won't ever be seeing him again.

CHAPTER TWELVE:

TROUBLE AT THE MILL

Over the next few weeks, Miriam became accustomed to a new way of life. She would rise at 5am to get dressed for the day. She would wrap her hair in a bun on top of her head and make her way to the room across the hall to check on Landon as he lay sleeping. She made sure his clean school clothes were laid out on his chair and that his satchel was properly packed and ready for the day. She would gently kiss Landon's forehead and whisper a prayer for him, before easing down the hall to the kitchen.

There, she would always find Ms. Martha stoking the cook stove with more kindling and keeping the biscuits warm and the coffee hot. Miriam thought to herself that no one would ever guess the heartache Ms. Martha carried inside because she had a strong faith that allowed her to sing, not sulk. It was Ms. Martha that had encouraged Miriam to read her Bible before work and she led the way by having her own Bible opened on the table each morning.

"You look tired, dear," Ms. Martha told Miriam, as she placed a cup of coffee and a warm biscuit with honey on the table. "You look lovely....but tired."

Miriam smiled, "I'm alright, Ms. Martha. I'm still getting adjusted to the new schedule. And I miss him. I miss him so much but staying busy keeps my mind on other things." Ms. Martha put her hand on Miriam's back and rubbed gently. "Yes, child. I can see where that would be the case. Sam would be so proud of you, Miriam. So proud," she said. Then she walked around the table to her Bible and flipped the pages to 2nd Corinthians 12. She read verse 9 to Miriam: And he said unto me, My grace is sufficient for thee: for my strength is made perfect in weakness.

As Ms. Martha turned back to the stove, Miriam remembered their recent conversation. Ms. Martha told her how difficult it had been when she and John, having been married for three whole years, still had no children. She had prayed and fasted, asking God to bless them with a child but still, no child came. They had practically given up when Ms. Martha found out she was expecting. The joy of that day was rivaled only when Merritt Phillip Long was born months later, just after midnight on October 3rd. Merritt quickly became the apple of his father's eye and was a smart, happy child as he grew up on the farm. Merritt excelled in everything he attempted and his future was bright. He talked openly with his parents about his dreams of going to university and becoming a doctor, after which he would return to the rural foothills area of his childhood and open a much-needed medical practice. Ms. Martha had worked tirelessly to help Merritt apply to two universities and to secure scholarships. Who could have imagined how everything would go so wrong? Before Miriam could complete her thoughts, she heard Mr. Reynold's truck pulling up the road. Realizing she was about to be late for her ride to work, she jumped up, grabbed her coat and scarf, and picked up her lunch pail. Just as she opened the door, she paused and ran back to give Ms. Martha a big hug. Spontaneously she said, "I love you, Ms. Martha!," and away she went, down the steps, and into the waiting truck.

After arriving at the mill, Miriam quickly set to work at the looms, where she had been assigned her job. She tried her best to mind her own business, work hard, and stay focused on the task at hand. But before noon, there was a commotion. Miriam looked up and saw the new secretary in tears, running from the office and out into the break yard. Soon, Mr. Greer appeared on the platform above the mill floor. He stood with his hands on his hips and a scowl on his face. Everyone in the mill feared Mr. Greer. the walking boss, because he was known to be harsh and demanding. He had the authority to hire and fire at will. Miriam didn't want to stare, so she went right back to work, focusing on the loom as she efficiently moved the shuttle. The clicking and whirring of the looms created a song all their own. Suddenly, Miriam heard a deep voice over her shoulder, "You!" Miriam lifted her eyes to see Mr. Greer standing over her shoulder.

"Stop what you're doing! You're coming with me," he barked. The color drained from Miriam's face as Mr. Greer grabbed her by the arm and pulled her up the steps.

CHAPTER THIRTEEN:

MIRIAM FINDS HER COURAGE

Mr. Greer shoved Miriam into the office and slammed the door behind him. Miriam immediately observed an office in full disarray. Folders were shoved into unclosed drawers, papers were strewn here and there, dust was on every surface, and the desk appeared as if it had never been properly set up for efficient work..

Mr. Greer spoke in a gruff voice, "Someone said you can type. Is that true?!"

"Yes...yes, I can," she answered softly. "I learned from a neighbor who lived down the road from me where I grew up. She worked as a secretary at a law office and..."

Mr. Greer interrupted. "I don't care about how you learned. And I don't care about your neighbor or your childhood! I just want this mess cleaned up! I haven't had a decent secretary in two years and I'm sick of it! Get in here and fix it. And if you don't work hard and get this job done, I will throw you out like the last girl...just try me and see!" He suddenly turned and marched out the door, leaving her alone with it all.

Miriam was fearful. She knew she couldn't afford to lose her job. She needed the income and jobs weren't easy to come by, especially not in a small town. She had never worked in an office. She had never managed books or handled billing or done any of things she imagined would be required. She was on the verge of tears when she heard something in her heart. She recalled something Ms. Martha had read just that morning from the Bible: "And he said unto me, My grace is sufficient for thee: for my strength is made perfect in weakness." Immediately Miriam felt the urge to pray. "Dear Lord, I'm scared. I don't know how to do this job because I've never done it. But Lord, if I can't do it, I will lose my work and my income. I won't have a way to take care of Landon. Please help me. Please show me what to do."

In that moment, Miriam felt the Lord guiding her, "Do what you know how to do. Do that first." When she opened her eyes, she thought to herself, "This place needs cleaning up and that's something I know how to do!" She began picking up trash, folding the newspapers, and collecting the files that were thrown about the room. She found some fabric scraps in a corner and took one to properly dust the desk, chairs, and cabinets. There on the desk was a photo of Mr. Greer, on his college graduation day, Miriam presumed. She took that photo into the inner office and placed it on Mr. Greer's own desk. She opened drawers and began to organize them. She filled the wastebasket with out-of-date notes and old scraps of paper. The strewn papers were old purchase orders that needed to be filed according to vendor. She found the filing cabinet and began to sort all of that out. Before she knew it, a couple hours had passed and she had to admit, the office was taking shape.

It was then that Mr. Greer appeared. When he entered the door, he stood in amazement at all Miriam had accomplished. He put his hands on his hips as he surveyed the clean surfaces. "That's more like it, little lady! Now get a legal pad and come in my office. You need to take dictation for a letter that needs sending." As Miriam reached for a pad and pen, she heard him barking, "Get in here, young lady! Hurry up! Move faster!"

Miriam had no idea how to dictate but she compensated and used her own methods to write quickly. Mr. Greer ended up dictating 2 letters and gave her instructions on several other office matters. He directed her to make a supply call and pull files for an order where there had been a misunderstanding. Miriam spent the entire afternoon attempting to finish the list he had given her. When her last item was completed, she knocked on his office door to let him know she was headed home.

Mr. Greer seemed pleased but he still maintained his irritable tone, as he said, "Well this is a start, little lady, but it only gets harder from here. You best show up bright and early in the morning and be ready to put in a long day. You might as well plan to eat lunch at your desk tomorrow because you will have a lot to catch up on!" While he spoke to her, he never made eye contact. Instead he looked in his middle drawer for a ruler and he even turned his back on her to search for a book from his bookcase. He ignored her presence as he continued to speak to her in a belligerent tone.

Miriam felt something she couldn't define come over her. When Mr. Greer finally took a breath, Miriam heard herself speak up. "Sir. Mr. Greer," she said firmly. He spun around in his chair to look at her. "Sir, I appreciate this opportunity to work in the office. I'm truly grateful. Mr. Greer, I want you to know I will do my very best. I will work hard for you and for this company. I am not afraid of hard work. And I will respect you. But sir....I expect you to respect me, too. My name isn't little lady. You may call me Miriam....or Mrs. Barker. I am a recent widow and mother to a little boy named Landon. I am a person, just like you, and I can't work in an environment where you scream at me and belittle me. That's something I needed to say. So....I will see you in the morning, ready to put in a hard day's work. Have a nice evening."

Mr. Greer sat like stone in his chair. For the first time that day, he was completely silent. He watched as Miriam moved quickly towards the door. But before leaving, she paused and looked back.

"And one more thing, Mr. Greer. Don't you ever again grab hold of me like you did today on the mill floor. Thank you, sir."

And with that she headed home and had no regrets.

CHAPTER FOURTEEN:

LANDON'S REQUESTS

Miriam's first few weeks working in the office provided her with new opportunities and challenges. She began to learn much more about why Mr. Greer was frustrated and gruff. Not only were all the records and files in complete disarray, but Miriam learned through Sarah and Beth Reynolds that Mrs. Greer was on bedrest at home. Sarah and Beth weren't gossiping when they told Miriam about her. They were simply letting Miriam know so she would have a better understanding of the circumstances. When the girls told her why Mrs. Greer was on bedrest, Miriam felt such compassion for the Greers that she immediately began to pray about ways she could help them.

In the midst of work demands, Miriam tried to help at home, too. She grew even closer to Ms. Martha and noticed that Landon had started giving Ms. Martha a hug each night before bedtime. One evening at the dinner table, Landon made an announcement. "Mama, Mr. John said he would be my grandpa. And I want him to. And that means Ms. Martha could be my grandma. And they said I could call 'em that....I could call 'em Grandpa and Grandma. They said I had to ask you first though, Mama. So can I? Can I, Mama?"

Miriam wasn't surprised at this development. Landon had truly captured the hearts of this sweet couple, and she could see by their smiles and darting eyes that they were pleased. "Well, Landon...if Ms. Martha and Mr. John say it's ok, then I think it's wonderful by me." Landon jumped out of his chair and ran over to hug Miriam tightly around the neck. But that hug didn't last long because he proceeded to hug Ms. Martha and finally John, who laughed out loud at Landon's enthusiasm.

That night at bedtime, Miriam made her way across the hall to help Landon say his nightly prayer. She noticed that he had become very quiet and almost solemn. She thought that was odd considering how excited he had been earlier in the evening.

"Is something bothering you, son?" she asked him.

"Well.....," Landon responded. "Maybe."

"Tell me. What is it?"

Landon took a moment before he answered and Miriam could tell he had a lot on his mind.

"It's Kenny, Mama. Kenny ain't...I mean, hasn't ....been to school this week and wasn't feeling good last time he was there. He don't have nothing to eat when he comes and I usually give him some of my lunch but he ain't been. I mean, he hasn't. And he said he ain't got no coat, Mama. And I wanted to get him one or somethin'. Can we, Mama....can we get him one?"

Miriam's heart was touched by Landon's concern for his friend, Kenny. She said, "I tell you what I'll do, Landon. Ms. Martha and I will ride out there where they've been staying and we will check on them. And I will make sure Kenny is ok and if he needs a coat, we will make sure he has one. Ok? And you recall what I told you, Landon, that whenever we are concerned about something, we should always pray about it?"

"Yes, ma'am, and I do, Mama. I pray about everything."

Miriam reached out and touched his hand. "I'm so glad, son. So let's pray for Kenny and his family right now."

Landon knelt beside his bed and began to pray: "Dear God, it's me Landon. And I'm here to pray about Kenny. And I'm worried cause I ain't seen him at school. And he needs stuff like something to eat and a warm coat. Please God, help him out. He's a real good friend. He's nice to everyone. Please help him out. And God, I know you remembered about when I asked you if you could give me some grandparents and you did. I got me a Grandpa and Grandma now. So thank you God for listening and letting me get Mr. John and Ms. Martha for grandparents. God please bless mama and keep her safe and tell daddy I love him. We sure do miss him down here. In Jesus' name, Amen."

It was hard for Miriam to hide her tears. Landon asked, "Did I say something wrong , Mama?" As she tucked the covers up under his chin, Miriam kissed his forehead. "Not at all, son. It's just that you make me so proud...and I love you."

Landon smiled, "I love you too, Mama."

Early Saturday morning, before Landon was awake, Carrie's car turned into the driveway. Ms. Martha's sister often visited early on Saturday mornings, bringing a book from the library for Ms. Martha to enjoy during the week. Once inside, Ms. Martha made her aware of the visit she and Miriam were getting ready to make to check on Kenny's family, and Carrie insisted on driving them. Soon after, the three of them made their way out just a few miles and down a narrow dirt roadway. When they rounded the corner, Miriam couldn't believe her eyes. A small shanty stood before them and appeared uninhabitable. "Well here we are," said Ms. Martha. "This is the old Peterson place. But this can't be right. I haven't been out this way in ages and it very much appears abandoned, Miriam. Are you sure this is where they are living?"

"That's what Landon said. I've even overheard Kenny mentioning the old Peterson place, so this must be it. But I'm not sure how anyone could live here, to be honest," Miriam answered, as she opened her car door to approach the house.

Miriam called out but no one answered as she continued walking towards the house. She pushed gently on the half-opened door and called out again, "Abigail...Abigail? Kenny? It's me...it's Miriam, coming to check on you." Once her eyes adjusted to the dark, she saw a sight she wouldn't soon forget.

"Hurry!! Hurry, Ms. Martha!! We need help!"

CHAPTER FIFTEEN:

THE OPEN DOOR

Miriam's eyes drifted across the battered floor of the old Peterson cabin, where she saw a rusty-framed bed and Abigail Ridge with both her children, Kenny and Catherine, huddled there under a thin blanket. There was no fire in the cabin, no pot simmering on the cookstove, and Miriam could feel the freezing chill in the air. She ran over to Abigail and saw that she appeared to be in a state of shock. Kenny and his sister Catherine were incoherent, pale, and clammy to the touch.

"He's not come back," Abigail muttered. "It's been two weeks and he's not come back. We ran out of food and....he's not come back." Miriam could see that Abigail was delirious with hunger and exhaustion.

Ms. Martha said, "Miriam....they are cold and starving. We must take them back with us. Let's get them to the car." One by one the ladies helped each one into Carrie's car and gathered what few clothing items were present in the cabin. Once back to Ms. Martha's, Miriam ran a tub of warm water and helped each one with a bath. Meanwhile, Ms. Martha readied Landon's room so that it could be used by Abigail and her children. Landon helped Ms. Martha put clean sheets onto his bed and he went upstairs to the linen closet and gathered extra blankets. Carrie worked in the kitchen, heating home-canned chicken soup and water for hot tea. Within a couple hours, Abigail, Kenny, and little Catherine, were well-fed and fast asleep in Landon's warm bed.

Early the following morning, Ms. Martha and Miriam sat in the kitchen and decided it was best for them to stay home from church services so they could attend to Abigail and the children. When Landon woke up, he insisted on staying home too, so he could talk to Kenny. But Miriam explained that Kenny needed time to feel better before talking or playing outside, and it was best for Landon to attend church with Grandpa and Phillip.

After a hot breakfast, Abigail explained that her husband Matthew had not had much success finding regular work. She had begged him to take a job at the textile mill. She pointed out that she could also work there and together, they would have a decent income. They could also get into a mill house, where there was working heat and the children could have small bedrooms and a better quality of life. But Matthew refused and left early one morning, saying he would be back in a few days with food for them but he had never returned. Miriam could see that Abigail was heartbroken and scared. Ms. Martha placed her arms around Abigail and hugged tightly. "Now listen here, child. There is no need to worry. We may not have the best of things but we have food, heat, a bed, and lots of love here. You can stay as long as you need. It will be a bit crowded, but we will make do just fine."

When Landon and the menfolk returned from church, Ms. Martha had the table laid out with chicken, potato salad, green beans, corn, fried apples, and biscuits. Kenny's face lit up when he saw Landon and they both filled their plates, sat at the small corner table, and laughed and told stories while they enjoyed their meal. They didn't go outside because Kenny was quite content to remain indoors, where he was safe and warm at last.

In the afternoon, Abigail talked more freely with Miriam, explaining that she was worried Matthew might never return. Things had been increasingly tense with Matthew and they had exchanged harsh words, as there was no money, food, or any prospects on the horizon.

WE HAVE THIS HOPE

She wasn't sure if her husband was depressed or simply overwhelmed, but despite her tearful pleas, he refused to do the most logical thing and work at the mill. With Matthew gone, Abigail knew she would need to find some way make ends meet and take care of two children, including one who was still a toddler and not yet in school. "I'm willing to work hard," Abigail said, "I just need an open door." Miriam understood those feelings very well. She had experienced them herself. But she could testify that God had provided for her and Landon in ways so generous and kind, that it was impossible not to share that kind of hope. "God will take care of you, Abigail. He will take care of you and the children, just as he did for Landon and me. He will never leave you or forsake you and you can depend on him. He will make a way."

On Monday when Miriam woke up, she immediately started praying about all the things on her heart and mind. She prayed for Abigail and the children. She prayed for Mr. and Mrs. Greer. "Dear Lord, we need you. We need an open door."

When Miriam arrived in the office, she could sense Mr. Greer was upset. "Apparently we need some part-time help at the company store." he groaned. "Things are a mess over there. And the truth is, I'm not even sure how much longer the store is going to remain open. The mill owners are talking about closing it soon, making it one less thing to maintain." Miriam could tell Mr. Greer had a heavy heart and it was something more than trouble at the store. She decided to speak up. "Mr. Greer...I want you to know that I would never discuss your personal business outside of this office. But, sir, I have been made aware of Mrs. Greer's condition. I know she is on bed rest in hopes of keeping the baby. And I just want you to know I have been praying for her...and also for you. I'm sure, after several previous losses, this is a very important time."

Mr. Greer remained quiet and had little to say. In that silent moment, God gave Miriam a wonderful idea. "Sir, I think God is working and he is already making a way for all our needs to be met."

Mr. Greer perked up. "What do you mean?" he asked.

"I think God is going to provide just the right person who can help us part-time at the store each morning and then go by your house and assist Mrs. Greer for a few hours each afternoon, helping with laundry, chores, and evening meal preparations. I realize this task would require someone who is kind, honest, and hardworking."

"I don't know, Mrs Barker," he responded. "It would take a special person to do all that and I'm not sure such a person exists."

"But she does, Mr. Greer, she does," said Miriam, smiling to herself at the beautiful sight of God's newly opened door.

CHAPTER SIXTEEN:

ABIGAIL'S ANSWERED PRAYER

Within the week, Abigail was well enough to go in each morning to the company store. She loved her new job, organizing goods and unboxing products. She also enjoyed seeing the customers and getting to know new faces. Abigail was grateful that Mr. Greer allowed little Catherine to come with her to the store. There was a small room off to one side, behind the counter, where Catherine could sit and color with crayons, look at books, and rest on a small cot.

After lunch, Abigail would walk a couple blocks towards Randolph Road. There, down a long driveway, was the beautiful two-story house where the Greers lived. Mrs. Greer was very quiet at first and didn't have much to say. Abigail wanted to ask more about the baby but sensed the time wasn't right. Despite some early awkwardness, however, she and Abigail found their bearings and developed a pleasant and professional relationship. While Catherine sat at the kitchen table playing with a homemade set of wooden blocks or counting little rocks she had collected in her pockets, Abigail learned her way around the house. She performed tasks such as sweeping, mopping, laundry, and cooking meals that would provide leftovers, making things easier for Mrs. Greer. Once Abigail completed her assignments, she would slip out just before Mr. Greer came home from work.

WE HAVE THIS HOPE

Miriam had arranged for Abigail to move into a mill house, where Kenny had his own modest room and Catherine stayed in the bedroom with her mother. The mill house was small but clean. It came with several furnishings and Abigail was thankful for them since she had nothing of her own to bring. There was a kitchen table with 4 chairs and a sofa with an end table. Both rooms had beds and Ms. Martha and Carrie had helped the family with sheets and blankets. The ladies of the church had been very kind too and packed a couple boxes with staples and home-canned foods to stock the pantry. With winter quickly approaching, the goods given were a gift from the Lord.

Abigail missed Matthew and thought of him every day. It hurt her heart to think he had walked away from them and chose not to return. She couldn't believe he would do something like that but Matthew hadn't been himself in the weeks leading up to his departure. Abigail also worried that something terrible had happened to him and that he was hurt or sick somewhere, away from the love and care of his family. All these scenarios brought her pain and anxiety. Mr. Long suggested they notify the local police about Matthew's disappearance so they could keep an eye out for him and the authorities had assured Abigail they would keep her informed. Other than this, there was nothing else she could do, except continue moving ahead, taking one day at a time.

On Thursday, as Abigail walked to work, she said a prayer of thanksgiving to God for all he had done for her. In a short time, he had strengthened her health, allowed her the comfort of a friendship with the Longs and Miriam, given her work and income, and provided her a safe place to live. "Lord," she said in her heart, "I had drifted away from you and from the closeness I felt to you when I was a young girl. And I was in a terrible state because of that. So thank you for not giving up on me....thank you for giving me a second chance to get close to you again. I wandered away like a sheep that gets out of the fold, but you came and brought me back in. And I hope I can do something good for you, Lord. That's my prayer. I want to be useful."

That morning, Abigail filled several requests for lamp oil and wicks. She helped two gentlemen find winter socks and gloves and she sold two brooms, one dustpan, and 3 boxes of matches. With Christmas approaching, women were getting ready for their baking and she filled several orders for flour and sugar. Her shift passed quickly that morning and soon it was time for her to make her way to the Greer's home. Abigail knew what lay ahead, as there were several clothing items that needed ironing and she hoped to scrub the kitchen sink. Mrs. Greer had mentioned the day before that she was in the mood for meatloaf and mashed potatoes, so Abigail had that on her to-do list, as well.

It was Thursday afternoon and Miriam was sitting at her desk sorting purchase orders. She was almost to the end of her paper stack and she was glad for it. When the phone rang, it took her a few seconds to answer. But when she did, she immediately heard the panic in Abigail's shaking voice.

"Miriam...it's me. It's Abigail. You need to hurry....It's Mrs. Greer, Miriam. I found her....in the bathroom floor, I found her. She's bleeding. Please hurry, Miriam. I don't know what to do....," Abigail pleaded, as Miriam dropped the receiver and fled down the steps.

CHAPTER SEVENTEEN:

MIRIAM'S HAPPY DREAM

Miriam and Abigail sat quietly on a bench in the waiting room, while Mr. Greer paced the floor. The tension was thick as they waited on an update from the doctor. They had been waiting for over an hour when Dr. Gantt rounded the corner and made his way over to them.

"Who is the person who found Mrs. Greer?" he asked abruptly.

"I was, sir," said Abigail softly.

"You can consider yourself a blessing, ma'am. By acting quickly, you saved her life today," Dr. Gantt told her.

A tear slid down Abigail's cheek as the doctor told them that Mrs. Greer was suffering from a low hemoglobin and had mostly likely become lightheaded, which caused her fall. She had been given a blood transfusion and received numerous stitches. She was also IV fluids since she was seriously dehydrated. Dr. Gantt recommended Mrs. Greer remain in the hospital on the maternity ward for the full two months until her delivery.

"So the baby...is it...ok?" Mr. Greer questioned.

"It appears so, Mr. Greer. But your wife needs extra care, so it's important she stays here until the time of her delivery," Dr. Gantt reassured him.

In the days that followed, Miriam did her best to keep everything running smoothly in the office. She even walked the mill floor occasionally and handled small issues that developed there. She remembered one of Ms. Martha's morning Bible readings out of Galatians which said: 'Bear one another's burdens and so fulfill the law of Christ.' Miriam felt she could assist Mr. Greer with his burdens by taking on extra work responsibilities wherever possible.

Miriam also worked tirelessly in the evenings, after all the house was quiet. Christmas was approaching and she had been working on several small projects. She has knitted Landon a new hat and scarf in his favorite color of blue. It had been Sam's favorite color too and her heart hurt to realize this would be their first Christmas without him. Sometimes Landon would talk about his daddy and she could sense how much Landon missed him. But Miriam recalled what Sam had often said: Life is for the living. She knew she couldn't let her grief take over her life, so she stayed busy and focused on working hard and raising Landon.

Miriam was almost finished working on the gift for Ms. Martha. She had talked it over with Landon and they had decided Ms. Martha needed a new apron. "I want Grandma's apron to have some flowers sewed on it, Mama. Can it, Mama? Grandma likes flowers and stuff, especially pink ones. Can you put flowers on it, Mama?" Landon's request was so sincere, it warmed her heart. This is why, despite her weariness after a long day's work, she took the handmade apron and embroidered extra detailing on it, including pink flowers with dark green stems and light green leaves.

For Grandpa, Miriam and Landon decided on warm pair of socks and for Phillip, Landon chose an orange fishing lure. Miriam had sewn a delicate handkerchief for Carrie, which she hoped Carrie would take with her to church on Sundays. Carrie, who was so quiet that she rarely spoke up, had once told Miriam, "There are everyday handkerchiefs and there are Sunday handkerchiefs. My Sunday handkerchiefs stay in a separate box because they are special." So she knew handkerchiefs were important to Carrie.

With the help of a monetary contribution by Ms. Martha, Miriam planned on purchasing gloves, peppermint sticks and gumballs for Kenny and Catherine. As for Abigail, Miriam and Ms. Martha had worked together to stitch a set of yellow kitchen curtains, complete with ruffles, from scrap fabric salvaged from the mill. Miriam had to admit they turned out beautifully and she knew Abigail would be excited to receive them. The only thing that remained was figuring out something to give the Greers and completing a couple small purchases for Landon with the bit of money she had been saving back from each paycheck.

At the end of the day when Miriam finally turned out the lights, she was so tired that she immediately fell into a deep sleep. One early December night, Miriam had a special dream. In the dream, she heard Ms. Martha's voice singing The Doxology and she saw a nurse, holding a beautiful baby in her arms. At first, she thought it was Mr. Greer's baby. But then she heard Ms. Martha say, "Look what God has done, Miriam. He has given you a baby!"

She heard her own voice saying, "Yes, he has! What a beautiful blessing!"

As she watched the nurse attend to the baby, Miriam felt her heart fill with immense joy and more contentment than she had ever known. Soon, she saw a handsome man who was unknown to her, yet familiar. He was beaming with pride and standing with his arm around Ms. Martha. His eyes were wet with emotion as Ms. Martha spoke out, "See Miriam? There is always hope...there is always hope in Christ."

With a startle, the alarm clock went off, jolting Miriam away from her dream. She lay in bed for a few moments, trying to reconcile what the dream meant. All she knew was the dream had been good. It made her happy. And Ms. Martha had been right. There is always hope in Christ, thought Miriam, as she stepped out of bed and into a brand new day.

CHAPTER EIGHTEEN:

GRANDMA'S IMPORTANT TRUTHS

A few days before Christmas arrived, Miriam found herself exhausted. She had worked overtime to keep things operating on schedule at the mill, while spending her evenings finishing up gifts and helping clean house and make preparations for the Christmas Day meal. Abigail, Kenny, and Catherine would be coming to the meal, along with Phillip, Carrie, and a farmer who lived a few miles to the west named Charles. Charles had no living family, so John and Ms. Martha invited him to join them.

Several years before, Charles' wife had gone to Tennessee to help care for her sick mother. One day she wrote Charles a letter to inform him that she would not be returning. Charles was heartsick and traveled to Tennessee to convince Teresa to come home to him, but she refused. "I never wanted to marry you in the first place, Charles," she had told him quite bluntly. "I just needed some security and you provided that. So I do appreciate it but now that my mother is settled here in Tennessee, I plan on staying here and starting a new life." Charles returned home to North Carolina, ashamed to tell his friends and neighbors the truth. It was Ms. Martha who figured things out and told John, "Go out there to Charles' farm and talk to him. He needs a friend." John wasn't too sure about that plan. "What am I supposed to say, Martha? Men don't talk like ladies do." But Martha insisted, saying, "Before you go, we will pray about it and God will give you the words." And sure enough, John had only been at Charles' farm for a few minutes when Charles broke down and told him the full story. From then on out, Ms. Martha liked to invite Charles to come over for holidays, as she figured he was awfully lonely.

Miriam thought of all the people she knew. Everyone of them had so many problems. Abigail had been abandoned by Matthew, or so it seemed. They hadn't heard one word from him since the day he left. Mrs. Greer, while

stabilized, was enduring a long hospital stay, trying to keep her baby from being born too early. Every hour was one more hour that the little one could develop and grow stronger before birth. Mr. Greer spent as much time as possible with her. He and his wife had been through so much pain over the years, desiring more than anything to have a child, and Miriam was in constant prayer for them. The Longs put on a strong front for others and there was no doubt their faith was great. But Miriam knew the heartbreak they felt over their severed relationship with their only child, Merritt, whom they hadn't seen in years. And Miriam herself was going through agonizing grief, missing Sam so badly and watching Landon prepare for his first Christmas without his dad. Lately, Miriam felt overwhelmed with it all. Maybe she was just tired or perhaps she was growing bitter. But she desperately wanted to blame someone for all the world's suffering and, more and more, she was tempted to blame God.

So on that Saturday afternoon, as Miriam worked in her room while feeling exhausted, she was thinking to herself, "Why should we celebrate Christmas anyway? No one is up for Christmas this year. It's really a waste of time and energy and I don't have an excess of either one of those things." As she was wrapping her packages in newsprint, she heard the kitchen door open and she heard Landon's excited voice.

"Mama, Grandma! We're back!! We found it," he called out. "Me and Grandpa and Phillip found the tree and it's really big. It's a good one!

And I helped chop it. Yes I did. I helped Phillip and Grandpa chop it cause I'm really strong now! And I helped carry it home, didn't I, Grandpa? Yes I did. I heaved it up and helped carry it home with the menfolk." Landon's voice continued to call out, until Miriam heard Ms. Martha racing down the hall, clapping with delight, "On Landon! It's magnificent! And you helped chop it? And you helped carry it? Oh my! Let me see your muscles. I tell you, you are growing like a weed. You will soon be as tall as the menfolk!"

Once the tree was in its stand, Ms. Martha asked Landon to help her keep it watered twice a day. Landon assured his Grandma that he was not only

strong but was also, "Reponsiple." Ms. Martha smiled at his newfound vocabulary. Landon ran back to his mother's room and knocked on the door. "Come on, Mama. Come see my tree I cut down." So Miriam tried to put on a happy face and made over the tree and how perfect it was. After a few moments, Miriam told Landon, "I am busy in my room so I need to go finish up in there. But I am very proud of your tree, Landon."

Landon said, unexpectedly, "Is daddy proud of my tree, Mama? Is he? Can he see my tree from up in heaven?" Miriam paused, as she tried to hide the tears filling her eyes. "I...I....I just don't know, Landon. But I figure he is," she stuttered, as she ran back to her room and quickly closed the door.

"Why is Mama upset, Grandma?" Landon asked.

"Well I imagine she is missing your daddy and sometimes when we are sad, we get upset, and we might even cry. And that is ok," Ms. Martha responded.

"Boys don't cry, Grandma! Boys are strong!" Landon insisted.

"Hear me now, little man. Boys do get sad and boys do cry. They may not feel comfortable showing their tears to everyone. But strong men do cry sometimes," Ms. Martha insisted. Landon looked at her in silence, as if he didn't believe her words. So Ms. Martha went on further. "Landon, do you know that Jesus cried? In the Bible it says that Jesus cried when his friend, Lazarus, died. And he cried again when he looked out over Jerusalem and saw that people were not living as they should and they were going to face big troubles because of it. So Jesus was just like you and me, Landon. He cried when he was grieving. Yet Jesus never sinned like we do, because he was God's Son."

From down the hall, Miriam continued to listen in on Landon's talk with Grandma, until soon, she was sitting in the floor near the closed door. She heard Landon's innocent voice and Ms. Martha's patient, grandmotherly voice, and such sounds made her feel melancholy.

"Grandma? I ask Mama about daddy being in heaven and stuff. But she always says she don't know the answer. And I just want to know, like....if daddy can see me and hear me and stuff."

Miriam could hear Ms. Martha take a deep breath. Then Ms. Martha spoke. "Landon, come sit next to Grandma. Let me tell you some important truths." Miriam heard Landon's steps going over to Grandma and in her mind, she could see Ms. Martha's arm around him. "You see, there are some things that we just don't know. We wish we did but we don't. God didn't tell us every detail about everything concerning heaven. But he told us what we need to know. When we have questions about things we don't know, we have to trust what we do know. And what do we know? We know heaven is a beautiful place, made just for us, to go and live forever with God. We know there is no night there! We know we won't cry there...and there will be no sickness or sadness. Doesn't that sound wonderful?! So that's what we know. And as far as what we don't know, that's where our faith comes in."

Miriam sat against the closed door in complete silence, as she felt the tears spill over. She listened intently as she heard Ms. Martha continue. "Faith is when we believe things we can't see because we trust in God's promises."

"But Grandma," Landon interrupted, "if we can't see it, how can we know it's true?"

"Do you believe the wind blows, Landon?" Ms. Martha asked him, as Landon shook his head.

"How do you know it blows, Landon? You can't see the wind."

Landon thought about that for a moment. "I can't see it but I can feel it! And I can see it blowing the trees around."

"That is true," Ms. Martha answered. "And who made the wind?"

Landon answered quickly, "God did! God made everything!"

"Yes he did. But we didn't see him make it. So how do we know?" Ms. Martha asked him.

"We believe it cause it's in the Bible. It says God made the world and stuff."

"That's right, Landon. So we learn in the Bible that God is over everything. He made the earth and he made heaven. And even if we don't have every answer, in faith we can trust that God does. And there is one thing we can always know, my child: God loves us and always will. He loves you and your mama and he loves me and Grandpa too. So when we can't know the answers to all our questions, we simply go back to what we do know. And we let our faith take care of the rest."

There was silence for a moment as Miriam sat in her room and wept out all her fears, exhaustion, and grief. Then Ms. Martha said one more thing.

"Landon, there is something I want you to always remember because it's very important in life: Never let what you don't know keep you from trusting in what you do know."

Miriam closed her eyes and repeated those words to herself: Never let what you don't know keep you from trusting in what you do know....

"Lord, when doubts fill my mind, remind me of what I know. I know that you love me. I know you want good things for me. I know you will never leave me. I know you will never fail me, Lord. Because you never have." Miriam whispered.

As she opened her eyes, Miriam heard the winter wind blowing outside her window. She decided it was time to dry her tears and join Landon in the living room, where he was excitedly gathering his handmade ornaments to place on the new tree.

CHAPTER NINETEEN:

GOD IS LOVE

After weeks of preparation, Miriam was relieved to wake up on Christmas Eve morning knowing all her hardest work was done. She had completed her gift making and gift buying. Everything was wrapped and ready to be placed under the tree. She had spent the previous day catching up on laundry and changing bed linens. It felt good to have some days off now that the mill was closed for the week.

As she pulled her hair into a bun and washed her face, Miriam glanced in the mirror and noticed that she was no longer the image of youth she once had been. Yes, she was still in her 20's, but life's challenges and hard work had left their mark. She pulled on her sweater and walked down the hall towards the kitchen, where she could hear Ms. Martha singing in her alto voice: "...Peace on the earth, goodwill to men, from heav'n's all gracious king; The world in solemn stillness lay to hear the angels sing..."

Miriam would never tire of that lovely voice. When Miriam rounded the corner, Ms. Martha paused and came over to embrace her warmly. "Good morning, my child. Happy Christmas Eve to you. I trust you slept well." Miriam agreed that she did, as she made her way to collect some coffee in her favorite cup.

"Today is a big day for us, dear. We will be rising the dough for cinnamon rolls, baking the pies, and bringing up some jars of canned goods from the cellar. Grandpa has us a delicious Christmas ham for our dinner tomorrow. And we will set the table for all our guests. It's such a joy to have a table full of loved ones this year," Ms. Martha smiled. "Oh yes, and let's not forget the Christmas Eve candlelight service at church tonight. It's one of my favorite services."

Miriam hated to admit she wasn't looking forward to it. She knew she would be vulnerable at such a poignant gathering and dreaded crying in front of the entire community. Ms. Martha noticed her silence and drew close to sit near her.

"My child, tell me," she said.

"Grandma. I just... I just dread being emotional. Christmas is meant to be a joyful time but for me it's also a sad time," Miriam confessed.

"Why of course it is!," Ms. Martha interjected. "Christmas is both happiness and sadness for everyone, my dear. But we must take the focus away from self and put it on the manger. Don't you know that the first Christmas was full of so many emotions? Mary and Joseph experienced things they never imagined! They were away from home, with no room where they could stay. Imagine Mary, feeling the labor pains coming, and knowing the Promised Child -the Messiah- was soon to be delivered...in a barn! I'm sure there were tears and fears and moments of the purest joy, one right after the other. Isn't that the way of life, Miriam? We can experience joy and sadness in the same breath. After all, there was a shadow over the manger. And that shadow was the cross. But that is what paved our way to heaven, isn't it? So every part of life is shadowed with others. But we must remember that God is over it all, Miriam...and his ways are ways of love." With that, Ms. Martha kissed Miriam on the head and returned to the stove.

Soon Landon was up and begging to go with Phillip and Grandpa to the barn. They were working on a secret project and Landon was feeling very proud to be in on it. "Mama, I'm gonna be working in the barn again with the menfolk. When boys get growed up, they can use tools and stuff. And they can do good things for the community and stuff and help people by surprisin' 'em and all. It's hard work but I'm strong, Mama. Grandpa said I was strong and useful. Didn't you, Grandpa?"

Grandpa said, "Absolutely! Why I don't know if I've ever seen another feller as strong at such a young age. I tell you he's a helper if they ever was one. I couldn't do without him. Could you, Phillip?"

Phillip tried to stifle a grin and said, "No sir, Mr. John. Landon's tough as a pine knot." Everyone's confidence in Landon caused him to sit taller in his seat and prompted him to take his last bite of oatmeal and announce, "Welp, it's 'bout time for the men to get to work. Work don't do itself, Mama!" And after hugging her tightly, Landon ran out the kitchen door, headed for the barn.

The day seemed to fly by and before long, supper dishes were cleared and everyone was freshening up for the Christmas Eve service. The ride over to the church was quiet and even Landon sat in silence. Miriam could sense that he was tired and would have no trouble getting to sleep for Santa to make his delivery.

The church looked serene in the bright moonlight, with the windows all aglow. Inside, Miriam waved at Abigail, who slid down to allow Landon and Kenny to sit side by side. During the service, different families stood to read portions of the Christmas story from Scripture and Miriam tried to do just what Ms. Martha had recommended. She focused on the manger. She focused on baby Jesus and wonder of his birth. When the time came for the candles to be lit, she stood with hers in hand and looked down the pew at all the love which surrounded her. There in the dark, illuminated by soft light, were the Longs, Phillip, Carrie, and Abigail. Across the aisle was the Reynolds family and other families she had gotten to know in the mill. She thought of all the trials the good Lord had brought her through and she felt her heart fill with more gratitude than she could ever convey. Joining together with the congregation, Miriam sang softly, "Silent night, Holy night, Wondrous Star, Lend Thy Light....With the angels let us sing, 'Alleluia' to our King, Christ the Savior is born! Christ the

Savior is born." When the song ended and the final prayer was offered up, everyone began to disperse and head home. Miriam was surprised at how peaceful she felt inside and how much she enjoyed staying to speak to everyone who had meant so much to her in the past year. Several mentioned Sam and how they missed him. She missed him too. So much.

Walking out the door of the church, Miriam stopped in her tracks when she saw it. Noticing it for the first time, lit by the moonlight across the pure white snow, Miriam saw the cross. She saw its long shadow falling across the churchyard.

"His ways are ways of love," she recalled Ms. Martha saying.

Yes, indeed, she thought.

God is love.

CHAPTER TWENTY:

HEAVEN AND NATURE SING PART ONE

Miriam opened her eyes to find Landon standing by her bed. "Mama, Mama....wake up," he whispered. "I think Santa done come, Mama."

"Landon! It's 5am," she protested.

"I know, Mama...but I think I heard the reindeer on the roof. And I laid real still and pretended to sleep for a long time. But I can't wait no more, Mama. Can you go see if he left me something?"

Miriam stepped out of bed and pulled on her robe. As she tiptoed down the hall, Landon waited, peeping out of her bedroom doorway. As she approached the living room she saw Ms. Martha stepping out of her room on the other side.

"I thought I heard a stir, dear child," Ms. Martha said. "He's up, isn't he?"

Miriam smiled. "Yes, of course. He heard the reindeer on the roof," she said.

"Let me get Grandpa up and get him in his slippers then. And I will put on the coffee," Ms. Martha said, scurrying to get things done.

Miriam leaned over to plug in the tree lights and she was surprised to see so many pretty packages under it. Despite the hard times surrounding the depression, God had blessed this family abundantly and met all their needs. They had good food, a comfortable home, and warm clothes. And greater than all that, they had one another.

Miriam returned to her room. "Santa did indeed come, Landon. But first you must brush your teeth and comb your hair."

"Aww Mama. Do I have to? Nobody cares about my hair." Landon rarely complained but Miriam could sense his anticipation.

"Yes, you have to, Landon. It won't take long and it will give me a chance to make up my bed...and hopefully yours too. Now get along and do as I said," she told him.

When all was ready, Miriam saw that Ms. Martha and John were waiting at the edge of the hall for Landon. They didn't want to miss one thing about Landon's first Christmas in their house. The expression on their faces was the same that was on Landon's: Pure Joy.

"Grandpa," Landon called out. "Mama said Santa done come and left me something."

"He surely did, young man. You musta been a good boy this year is what I say," John replied.

As Landon rounded the corner, his eyes were bright as stars. John took the lead and said, "Landon, in our house we never open presents until we have read the Christmas Story from the Good Book. Christmas is about Jesus. Jesus coming to earth was the best gift of all. And we always want to remember his birthday before we do anything else. So bring me my Bible, son." When Landon had brought it from the kitchen table, he climbed in Grandpa's lap and listened to the story about the manger and the swaddling cloths and there being no room in the inn. And he listened as Grandpa read about the shepherds and the angels and the wise men and the star.

WE HAVE THIS HOPE

When the Scripture was finished being read, Ms. Martha said, "Grandpa, we should sing a song for Jesus' birthday. What shall it be? What do you think, Landon?"

"Joy to the world!" Landon exclaimed. "I love that one, Grandma. It says the Lord is come and He rules the world and stuff. And it says heaven and nature sing. And I was wonderin' about how nature sings, Grandma. I don't know."

"Well," Ms. Martha started out, "that's a great question, Landon. God created nature. He made the trees and oceans. He made the rocks and hills. He made all the heavens, with the clouds and the sun and the moon..."

"And the stars!" Landon interjected with excitement. "I love the stars, don't I, Grandpa?"

"Oh yes you do. Why, I don't know if I've ever seen a boy that loves a good star like you do, Landon."

Grandma continued, "So nature sings by doing its best at whatever God created it to do! The flowers bloom in spring and the snow falls in winter. The leaves turn colors in the fall and the ocean tides come in and then go out, just as God instructed them to do, Landon. And yes, the stars come out at night!"

"So the bright star that led the wise men was singing," Landon said. "It was doing what God told it to do and it was taking the wise men to Jesus!"

"That's right, Landon. And all of heaven and nature rejoiced at the birth of Jesus!"

Soon the whole living room was full of voices, singing about joy coming to the world.

"Is it time, Mama? Is it time for presents now?" Landon asked.

"I suppose it is, son," she answered.

Miriam was very proud of how Landon carefully opened his gifts and appreciated each one. He loved the blue hat and scarf she made for him and asked, "Can I wear them to school or just to church?" And Miriam assured him he could wear them to both school and church and Landon was happy with that answer.

From Santa, Landon received crayons and a coloring book with pictures of horses in it. He also received a small toy tractor that fit nicely in his pocket and a stocking with new socks, two new pencils with erasers, a tangerine, an apple, a pack of bubble gum and several chocolate drops.

Landon's present from Grandma and Grandpa was in a big box. It was wrapped in red paper with gold stars on it. They all watched as he took his time opening it, removing the tape with care. When he lifted the lid off the box, he screamed out with delight! "Look, Mama, look! I got me a cowboy hat, Mama! I got one all my own and nobody else's!" Landon ran to hug John and Ms. Martha, who were beaming from ear to ear.

Grandpa said, "Landon...keep looking in the box. There's something else!"

Landon ran back to the box and lifted the white tissue paper to find a lasso.

Miriam could hardly contain him, he was so thrilled with all his gifts.

"I'm going outside Mama. I need to get my coat on. I gotta go work the farm. Some stuff needs catching with my new lasso."

As Landon ran down the hall to his room, Miriam stayed back and hugged Ms. Martha and John. "Thank you," she said softly. "You have blessed us so much and we are grateful." Ms. Martha let the tears slide down her face. "My child," she said, "YOU have blessed us. More than you'll ever know. Isn't that right, Grandpa?"

"Oh yes it is. Truer words have ne'er been spoken, is what I say," affirmed John.

About that time, Landon appeared in the living room, his cowboy hat on his head and his lasso in hand. He ran straight through for the back door and outside he went to have a fun, Christmas Day adventure.

Under the tree sat presents for others. Miriam had a few with her name on them, as well. But they would wait. For now, there was cinnamon rolls coming out of the oven and hot coffee percolating on the counter. It would be nice to sit and enjoy the quiet.

Ms. Martha was about to get started with her Christmas Day kitchen duties when the phone rang. There were very few phone calls that came out to the Long's farm, so the sound of it startled Miriam and reminded her of when Sam was sick. John went to answer the call and Miriam and Ms. Martha stood completely still as they listened.

"Oh no," Mr. John said.

"I see," he continued. "Of course we will pray."

He paused to listen again. "I know. I know," he said, "but we must put our trust in God. Try not to worry now. We will be there shortly."

He returned the receiver to the hook and slowly turned to look at Ms. Martha. His voice was firm and unwavering.

"It's an emergency. Get the boy inside and let's quickly ready ourselves. We're going to the hospital."

CHAPTER TWENTY-ONE:

HEAVEN AND NATURE SING PART TWO

John led his family down the hospital hallway. As soon as Mr. Greer saw them, he stood up and hurried to meet them. Miriam had never seen Mr. Greer looking so distraught, with his clothes disheveled and his eyes strained with exhaustion.

"Thank you for coming," Mr. Greer said. "She's been back there for a while and no one has come out to tell me anything."

"Now, now, Mr. Greer, you mustn't fret. Firstborn babies simply take forever to finally appear," Ms. Martha assured him.

"But it's far too early, Ms. Martha. Ginny had at least 5 weeks to go," Mr. Greer said, rubbing his forehead intently.

Miriam thought back to Landon's birth and how calm Sam had been. His patience had helped her tremendously.

"Mr. Greer, have you eaten? We packed you some warm cinnamon rolls and a thermos of coffee. You need to keep your strength up," she said.

While Mr. Greer sat with John and tried to eat, Ms. Martha used the hospital phone to call her dinner guests to let them know what was happening. Soon, all her guests were arriving at the hospital to await the birth of the Greer's new baby. Abigail arrived with Kenny and Catherine and were happy to see Landon. The children huddled together at the end of the hall, talking about the things Santa had brought. A bit later, Carrie came, bringing sandwiches and cookies. Finally, Charles and Phillip arrived and took their place along the wall where the men were gathered.

Time passed slowly. Standing near the window, Miriam could see the snow clouds beginning to gather. Just at that moment, Dr. Gantt came bounding out into the hallway, headed straight for Mr. Greer.

The doctor extended his hand and said, "Congratulations sir! You have a son! Both mother and child are doing well, although we have taken the baby to the nursery to keep a close eye on him for a little while. He is small but mighty. He has a good, strong cry. A nurse will come out shortly to take you back to see your wife and to visit the nursery."

Mr. Greer broke down in tears of joy and relief. He had a son....on Christmas Day. There was great relief and thanksgiving as they all witnessed prayers being answered. Everyone wanted to stick around until Mr. Greer came back out to give them a full report and all were overjoyed to see his bright smile.

"Come to the nursery window and meet our son: Gregory Luke Greer, the Second. He's the handsomest boy I've ever seen! We will call him Luke." Mr. Greer was aglow with pride over his namesake and no one could blame him. He had waited for this moment for a very long time. They all peeked in the nursery window, the children clambering on tippy toes to get a good look. He was tiny and perfectly beautiful and Ms. Martha cried and cried.

Mr. Greer reassured everyone that Mrs. Greer was doing well. All the anxiety of the delivery had left her exhausted but she was also ecstatic that their little boy had arrived, safe and sound.

After spending a good bit of time chatting and admiring the new baby, John announced that it was time for the visitors to head home and let the Greers get some rest. Ms. Martha told everyone, "We didn't get to share our Christmas meal today but we will most certainly reschedule. If everyone can attend tomorrow, we will do it then." Everyone agreed that time would work for them.

Each one gathered to hug Mr. Greer or shake his hand. What an exciting day it had been and it made for a Christmas that would long be remembered. As they walked down the hall to go, Landon suddenly turned back. "Mr. Greer! Mr. Greer, wait!"

Landon approached him and Mr. Greer knelt down to speak with him. "Mr. Greer, I brought baby Luke a present," Landon said, as he pulled a wooden star from his pocket. "My grandpa's been teaching me how to whittle with his folding knife and we made Christmas stars. He done most of the carvin', Mr. Greer, but I did a little bit. And I sanded the edges real good. Grandpa said I'm real good at sanding stars and stuff. And I was thinking to give Luke this star we made. Baby Jesus had a star and I thought Luke could have one too. Cause Luke's done got the same birthday as the Lord in the manger." Mr. Greer's eyes filled with tears as Landon pushed the wooden star into his hand and ran out into the snowy evening to head home with his family.

CHAPTER TWENTY-TWO:

HEAVEN AND NATURE SING LANDON'S ADDENDUM

The ride home from the hospital was adventurous. The snow began blowing in hard and collecting on the roadway. Ms. Martha worried for just a moment about what might happen if a heavy snow were to postpone her Christmas dinner once again. But her heart was too full of joy to be overly concerned about it.

As they rounded the last bend in the road, Miriam spotted the kitchen light in the farmhouse window and felt thankful to finally be arriving home. It had been a full day and she was tired, but happy.

When the car pulled in the driveway, Landon was the first to jump out. He had left his cowboy hat and lasso at home and he was excited to run to his room and see them again. But when he approached the kitchen door to go inside, there was a package propped up at the top of the steps. It was wrapped in white and had a bright red bow attached. In the upper right corner, Landon read his own name. "TO LANDON."

"Look Mama! Here's a gift with my name on it!"

"Well goodness, it is, Landon! I wonder who left you a package? Let's pick it up and bring it inside," Miriam said.

Landon placed the gift on the table as everyone began removing their hats and gloves. Ms. Martha started taking out the ingredients for her hot cocoa as Miriam carried their coats to the closet. Soon, the whole family was gathered in the kitchen to watch Landon unwrap his surprise present.

Landon quickly removed the red ribbon and pulled on the tape. When he unfolded the wrappings, he saw a beautiful Holy Bible.

"Wow! It's a brand new Bible, Mama! I ain't never had my own Bible! Is it from you, Grandma?"

"It's not, Landon," she answered.

"How about you, Grandpa?," Landon asked.

"No, son," Grandpa said, "it's not from me. But it sure is a nice Bible. It's one of the nicest Bibles I've ever seen."

Miriam reached down to touch the soft leather cover. "You should open the cover, Landon. Maybe there's a name in there," she suggested.

Landon's little hands carefully turned to the dedication page and Miriam immediately drew in an audible breath.

"It says it's from Daddy, Mama. Look, Look!," Landon exclaimed, pointing to the words on the page. "It's from Daddy but....how? Daddy's in heaven. How did Daddy bring me a Bible from heaven?," Landon asked, looking at his mother and then his grandma.

Miriam was unable to speak so Grandma stepped closer.

"Landon, I don't know the exact answer. But you have to remember that just like God did miracles in the Bible days, he does miracles now. And sometimes our faith has to work extra hard when there are things we don't understand. That's when we have to trust God even more."

As Miriam's tears flowed down, she touched the dedication page, where she read the words:

To Landon

From Daddy

Christmas Day 1938

As she looked closely, she realized there was something behind the dedication page, so she turned it to find a folded letter.

"What's that, Mama?"

"It's a letter to you, Landon," she whispered.

Seeing that Miriam was overcome with emotion, Grandma said, "Would you like me to read it to you, Landon?"

"Yes, yes, Grandma!"

Miriam passed the letter to Grandma and quietly sat down next to Landon, as Grandma read aloud:

"Dearest Landon,

When you read this note, I'll be in heaven with Jesus. I'm sure there will be a big celebration for such a wonderful day, the day we recognize Jesus' birthday. I know the angels will be singing and I will be singing too.

I wanted to give you a special gift for Christmas, son, and the Holy Bible is the most special gift I know. I hope you will take it and read it everyday. Inside, you will find God's most important lessons for life. If you read it, study it, and always keep it in your mind, you will be wise. If you do what it says, you will be strong and blessed.

Landon, I hope you will always keep love in your heart because love never fails.

I hope you will always remember how much I love you, Landon, and how much I love your mama. I have no doubt God is taking care of you both and I know he always will. He will lead you so be sure to follow him. He will open new opportunities for you and bring new people into your life. Make room for them. Love them and let them love you.

I am proud of you, Landon.

Merry Christmas Son.

Love,

Daddy"

The room was silent as Landon picked up the Bible and held it close in his arms. Then, looking up towards heaven, he said:

"Thank you, Daddy. Thank you for the Bible. I'll take good care of it, Daddy, and I'll read it like you said. Me and Mama sure do miss you down here. I wish I could see you. But I hope you're having fun singing with the angels in heaven.

Merry Christmas, Daddy. I love you."

At that very moment, Landon reached out and took his mother's hand. "Hey, Mama, I just thought of somethin'. Grandma was right! Heaven and nature REALLY DO sing, Mama. They really do. Heaven and nature sing...."

CHAPTER TWENTY-THREE:

TIME TURNS

Miriam dressed by the soft lamplight, moving quickly because the house was cold. The snow from a few days before was almost gone but even so, a chill lay over every surface. Miriam's mind was set on spring and she couldn't wait to see the first sign of new life on the farm. The daffodils would soon be lifting their bright faces to the sun and her heart raced at the thought.

January had passed in a blur. Work in the office was busier than ever but the atmosphere was surprisingly pleasant. Mr. Greer seemed like a different man once he became a father. He became kinder and more understanding of the mill workers. He would call them by name when he went down on the mill floor and he would ask about their families and how they were getting along. Baby Luke had certainly changed his life, and in a good way.

At the breakfast table, Miriam made note of the fact John was not yet up for the day. Matter of fact, John had missed several mornings at the table lately and Miriam was worried about him. Landon noticed too and spoke up.

"Grandma, why's Grandpa not eatin' with us?"

Ms. Martha smiled softly and said, "Well son, I reckon he's extra tired these days and his bones ache in this chilly air. But never you mind, Grandpa will be up shortly to get his gravy," she reassured him.

"Guess what, mama?," Landon asked. "Phillip's gonna let me hook up the tiller on the tractor! Grandpa done told him it was nigh time I learned to work the garden and get it ready for spring plantin', ain't that right, Grandma? And I'm gonna make some rows and put down some seeds and stuff, ain't I, Grandma? And I can grow corn taller 'n me!" Landon was very excited and talking so fast, no one else could get in a word.

Ms. Martha chuckled and her laughter made Miriam laugh too. There was no doubt Landon was cut out for farming. "I believe farmin's in his blood," John had said not too long ago, leaning back with his thumbs hooked onto his overall straps. "Yep. God's done gave me a little farmer," he beamed with pride, and Miriam had thought to herself how blessed she would be if Landon grew up to be as fine a man as his grandpa. John worked hard, lived out a strong but quiet faith, was good to his family and neighbors, and he was generous to those in need.

It was later that afternoon when Mr. Greer mentioned the company store. He said the mill owners were going to close it and it was something Miriam dreaded to hear. She knew Abigail depended on the store job, not only for the income it provided, but also because it allowed her to live in the mill house.

Abigail had made a good life for her family there over the last several months. Every time Miriam stopped by the house for a visit, she was impressed with how much Abigail had done with what little she had. Abigail would babysit on the weekends in exchange for an old end table or a hand-me-down rug. She would clean whatever she acquired and add polish or paint or mend tattered hems. The pretty curtains Miriam had stitched and given her for Christmas were pressed perfectly and adorned the kitchen windows. Where would Abigail go if she lost the mill house?

When Miriam voiced her worries, Mr. Greer assured her he already had a plan in mind. But before they could discuss that plan, Mrs. Greer called. Immediately Miriam knew that something was wrong and she was concerned that the baby might be sick.

"We're on our way to the hospital right now, dear. Don't worry. Just pray," he said. As he hung up the phone, he stood quickly, grabbing his jacket and hat.

"Let's go, Miriam. Get your things."

"Oh no," Miriam said softly. "Is everything ok with baby Luke?!"

"Luke is fine, Miriam. It's Abigail. Ginny said the police came by while Abigail was there helping with the afternoon chores."

Miriam stopped in her tracks. "The police? What in the world?!," she exclaimed.

Mr. Greer looked back to Miriam, even as he kept moving towards the door. His countenance was grim.

"It's about Matthew. And it's not good news."

CHAPTER TWENTY-FOUR:

WHEN GOD MAKES A FAMILY

Officer Jenkins greeted Mr. Greer and Miriam as they entered the Emergency Room. Miriam was on the verge of tears and he reached out and patted her arm. "Ms. Miriam," he said, "it's going to be alright. Ms. Abigail is ok, she's just had a shock is all."

Officer Jenkins pulled Mr. Greer and Miriam into a small room so they could have some privacy. "Truth is, we heard from a department over in Fairview, South Carolina, this morning. Abigail's husband, Matthew, died there in a house fire yesterday. They were able to get the fire put out, but both Matthew and the homeowner, a woman named Inez Deaton, suffered from severe smoke inhalation, which unfortunately claimed their lives."

Miriam tried to process the information in her mind but she was struggling. "So...Matthew was...with a woman....in the house fire?" Officer Jenkins knew exactly what she was asking. "Unfortunately yes, Ms. Miriam. And I know that news is quite disturbing to Ms. Abigail. From what we can gather, Inez Deaton was a fairly well-to-do lady. A good ten years older than Matthew, it seems. And she had....taken him under her wing," he said, looking down at the green tiled hospital floor.

Miriam's thoughts were spinning, as Mr. Greer turned his back to look out the window. How could Matthew leave his family and never reach out to them, just to let them know he was alive and well? How could he take up with another woman this way and betray sweet Abigail, who was working so hard to take care of their children on her own? Her heart was broken for her friend.

"I want to see her," Miriam said to Officer Jenkins. "I want to get back there."

"Well that's not up to me, but I will be glad to go find a nurse and let the staff know you are here, as Ms. Abigail's friend," the officer said.

"I'm her family, Officer Jenkins. I'm family. And I insist on going back to see her," Miriam said, as Officer Jenkins nodded and made his way out into the hallway.

Miriam and Mr. Greer stood in silence, until a nurse came to the door and said, "Mrs. Barker, you can come with me and I will take you to the patient's room." Before she left, Miriam walked over to Mr. Greer, who was still looking out the window. "Please pray for me," Miriam told him. "I don't know what to say....I don't know how to comfort her. I...I'm not sure....," she said, as her words drifted away.

Mr. Greer never turned from the window, but Miriam listened as he spoke. "I have been far from God, Miriam. In the past. I have doubted him. I've cursed him, I'm ashamed to admit. But he's never abandoned me. He's never left me or betrayed me. And he won't betray you either, Miriam. He's with you and will give you the words." A tear slid down Miriam's cheek. That was the first time she had ever heard Mr. Greer talk about his relationship with God. And what he had to say was just what she needed to hear.

"Thank you, Mr. Greer. Thank you for reminding me," Miriam said as she turned to go.

Abigail's room was dark, with only a small bit of light coming in, but Miriam could hear her sniffling. Abigail was seated on the bed, her shoulders and head down. Miriam quietly moved over and sat beside her. Silently, she slid her arm around her friend's shoulder, and together they cried. After a few moments, Miriam gathered the courage to speak.

"Abigail. I'm not going to speak about Matthew. That's not for me to do. I'm sure you have plenty enough that you could say about him. But I will speak instead about Jesus. During my darkest days, Jesus took care of me. He put me with the right people. He provided for everything I needed and that Landon needed. He was with me in my grieving and brought me comfort somehow. His Word became my guide and when my mind would fill with negative thoughts or anxious feelings, I would just get out my Bible and start reading it. It kept me going, one more day. I don't have all the answers, Abigail. But Jesus does. When your world is crashing down, he will hold you together. He will never leave you. He will never betray you. He will always be there for you...because he loves you more than anyone on earth ever can."

Abigail didn't utter a word, but leaned into Miriam's embrace and nodded her head in agreement. Finally, Abigail said, "I don't know what to do next. I don't know how to tell Kenny. Catherine's young and she won't understand. But Kenny....," she cried softly.

"I think you should be as direct as you can, without the need to give too much information, Abigail. And I will be glad to stand with you as you tell him, if you want. Because we are family now. We are sisters. I never had a sister and always wanted one. So I consider us sisters and sisters are there for each other, no matter what. Right?,"Miriam said.

Abigail smiled slightly, "Right."

"I'm ashamed to say this...real ashamed, Miriam. But..I've got no money to pay for the burial. Do you think they will let me make payments on it," Abigail asked, as her tears resumed.

"There's no need to worry 'bout that." Miriam and Abigail heard a strong and familiar voice speaking from the doorway

"It's already taken care of child," John spoke. Never was a more welcome sight seen than in that moment. Just behind him came Mrs. Martha, rushing past him with her arms open wide.

"They didn't want to let us back. They said it would be too much of a disturbance. But there is no way they can keep us from our dear girls. Our Miriam and our Abigail. Isn't that right, Grandpa?," Ms. Martha asked, looking back.

John put his thumbs in his overall straps and said affirmatively, "That's exactly right, Grandma. No one will keep us from our daughters is what I said. And you might as well gather your things and come on home with us for a spell, Abigail. Why, we got plenty o' room for everyone and you can stay as long as you like. And we will get our grievin' done together as families do, at least the first of it anyhow. And we will see to the funeral service and get that behind us as a family, too."

Ms. Martha then spoke softly to Abigail, as she held firmly to her hand. "Now let's not go jumping to conclusions about Matthew. He was wrong not to call you and the children. He was wrong to leave and not send home supplies. He did lots of things wrong. But we just don't know what was in his mind. We don't know what was in his heart. We have to leave that to the Good Lord. So what we have to do instead is think on what's good, if we can find some. The way I see it, the good thing about Matthew was that he had a lovely wife, who is strong and capable. The Bible says a virtuous woman is worth more than rubies. Matthew was rich. His wife was good to him all the way to the end of his days, and that's saying a lot. And Matthew was blessed with two wonderful children. He had a loving son in Kenny and a precious daughter in Catherine. It seems to me the best part of Matthew is right here in our community. Don't you think so, Grandpa?"

"Oh you better believe it. I say the best part of Matthew is right here and gonna be here for years to come. And that's what I'm proud of, that we get to be here with 'em and watch 'em grow up and do the good things God's got laid out," John said.

And so it was that Abigail became Miriam's sister. And Abigail became John and Ms. Martha's daughter, right alongside Miriam. And Catherine and Kenny became cousins to Landon, and they never considered themselves in any other way all the days of their lives.

Because just like it says in the Bible, God puts the lonely in families.

CHAPTER TWENTY-FIVE:

BEST NURSE EVER

Matthew's funeral was brief and Abigail held up as best she could. She focused on being strong for the children, even though they had shed no tears.

Miriam had sat in Abigail's living room as she told Kenny and Catherine about their father's death. "He was living in a house that had a fire and he breathed in smoke while he was sleeping. So even though the firemen were able to get the fire out, daddy's lungs were damaged by smoke. I know this is very sad news. But we will get through this difficult time by trusting in Jesus and relying on the kindness of our friends. Do you have any questions? You can ask or say anything you like." Kenny looked down at the floor while Catherine clung to her doll, but neither had anything to say. Abigail then explained they they would be spending a week or so with the Longs, out on their farm. Kenny's face brightened when he realized he would be on the farm with Landon, where they could play and explore.

When Miriam returned to work, she expressed her worries to Mr. Greer.

"Mr. Greer...how will you ever tell Abigail about the mill store closing? She will be devastated. I haven't slept well for several nights because I'm so concerned. Abigail doesn't need extra burdens just now, not with the circumstances surrounding Matthew's death."

"You don't have to worry Miriam. I've got everything worked out," Mr. Greer responded.

"But how?" Miriam asked, wringing her hands.

"Aren't you always the one telling others to trust in God? Have you quit trusting him to make a way?"

Mr. Greer's question brought her back to reality. He was right. In this situation, her faith was wavering.

"You're right, Mr. Greer. I've been so overwhelmed with helping Abigail, that I haven't prayed things through as I should."

"It's ok, Miriam. You have been an incredible friend to Abigail. And she has been a big blessing to me and my family. That's why I've worked something out. Want to hear it?" After Mr. Greer explained it all, Miriam had to take a tissue to wipe away her tears. She was filled with both relief and excitement. She prayed in her heart, "Thank you, God, for making a way for my sweet sister."

"When will you tell her about this?," Miriam asked Mr. Greer.

"There's no time like the present! Should we call her into the office?" Miriam nodded in agreement and within the hour Abigail was seated in Mr. Greer's office, with Miriam sitting next to her for support.

Mr. Greer began, "Abigail, I know this has been the toughest of times for you and the children. And you are still grieving and will be for a while. So that is why I haven't wanted to tell you additional bad news. But I can't put it off any longer. The mill store is closing." Abigail took in a quick gasp but tried to hide it. Even as her eyes filled with tears, she said, "I understand, Mr. Greer. I will begin looking for other living arrangements right away."

Mr. Greer continued. "Well, there's something else I wanted to speak to you about. You have been a wonderful help to Ginny and me. You have assisted us through a critical pregnancy and your quick actions saved the lives of both Ginny and baby Luke. We could never thank you enough. When Ginny was in the hospital, you went up there everyday to help out, because the hospital is shorthanded. Everyone there was impressed with your ability to work efficiently and to quickly learn skills. One of the nurses happened to tell me that you would make an excellent nurse yourself and that you had expressed an interest in becoming a nurse, but you felt it was impossible, because of your home obligations. Is that true?"

Abigail was following Mr. Greer's words attentively. "Yes, sir, it is. There is no possible way I could go off to nursing school. I need to provide for my children. I'm the only parent they have," she said softly.

"There's another way, Abigail," Mr. Greer said. Abigail looked at Miriam, who was smiling from ear to ear. "I spoke with the nursing director and if you are willing to dedicate three years of service to the hospital, they will pay you a salary as you are training. In other words, you will receive nursing education on the job and will earn your full certification upon completion of your training. It isn't easy. It's a demanding effort that sometimes will require you to work at night or on weekends. Miriam has agreed to help all she can with your children on those occasions, and Mrs. Greer has offered to help, as well."

"You mean...I could...work at the hospital, get paid, and also receive nurses' training?," Abigail asked in disbelief.

"That's right," Mr. Greer said, "And I spoke to the director about your housing issue. I agreed to let you keep the mill house if you will dedicate 6 hours a week in the mill's elementary school. That's 2 hours, 3 days a week. The hospital has agreed to supervise you. You will teach the children about good nutrition, exercise, and hygiene. You will be available to assist students with their health. The rest of your working time will be spent training in the hospital. Does this arrangement sound agreeable to you?"

Through tears of joy, Abigail answered, "This is more than agreeable. I can't believe what I'm hearing. This is a dream I've had since childhood but I knew it could never be. So thank you. Thank you so much, Mr. Greer, and also to Mrs. Greer. And praise be to God. He heard my prayer and he answered in ways I never thought possible."

As Abigail dried her tears, Miriam thought to herself what a good man Mr. Greer had turned out to be. Abigail had given the best of herself to help Mr. and Mrs. Greer, and now they were giving back to her.

Miriam smiled and wrapped her arm around the precious young lady that she considered a sister. "You're going to be a nurse, Abigail. And what an amazing nurse you will be. You'll be the best nurse ever," Miriam said, as the afternoon sun beamed through the second floor window of the Ora Textile Mill.

CHAPTER TWENTY-SIX:

THE CALL

Miriam looked out over the landscape from the kitchen window. She was thankful the deep winter days were behind them, as she saw the daffodils lifting their bright faces to the early spring sun. March had finally arrived and she was encouraged by the longer sunlight each day. Landon was also full of excitement and looking forward to getting his hands in the dirt. Sections of the garden were already being prepared for plantings of lettuce, cabbage, beets, radishes, peas, and turnips.

Miriam turned as Ms. Martha entered the kitchen from the hallway. She noticed Ms. Martha looked tired but that was to be expected. Ms. Martha worked tirelessly around the house. She was constantly cleaning, cooking, baking, tending to Landon and helping him with homework, mending, sewing, and preparing dishes to take to those who were sick or grieving.

"I was thinking, Grandma, that I might ask Mr. Greer if I could take a few days off work. That way, I could help with the spring cleaning you've talked about. I know there's so much to do....,"Miriam trailed off.

"Oh no, my dear. That's not needed. I will have no trouble at all doing it. I might take things a step slower this year though. I was thinking of starting here in the kitchen this week, taking down the curtains for washing and giving them a nice press. And I need to take all the spices and herbs out of the pantry and give everything there a good wiping down with some hot soapy water. And then I could move over to the hutch. It's a sight! I'll take out all the dishes and give everything a fresh polish. And then I will go through the paper drawer and sort and organize that again because it's so easily shuffled around and disorganized. And my baking cupboard is so out of sorts since we made all those winter goodies. I need to take everything out and get that back in order. And I will get these rugs up and hung over the line for a firm beating. They need the bright sunshine and fresh air to get them sanitized. And while the rugs are up, I will get out the bucket and brush and get these floors scrubbed down. They desperately need it!"

"Goodness, Grandma! You've worn me out just talking about all that needs doing!" Miriam exclaimed.

About that time, Landon came in the kitchen door, hurriedly wiping his dirty boots. "We got eggs, Grandma! We got 10 eggs! Phillip told me to bring 'em in but I can't stay cause we gotta clean up the coop and get the chickens their water. And we gotta do lots of stuff and I can't stay but here's the eggs and I'll be back to eat somethin' in awhile but right now I got farmin' stuff to do so bye. Love you," he said in a rush, hardly taking a breath, before flying back out the door.

Miriam had to laugh at the handsome young farmer Landon was becoming. Moving in with John and Ms. Martha had been one of the best things to ever happen to them.

"Time for me to head out, Grandma. I need to be in the office early this morning, so I will just take a biscuit with me and be on my way," Miriam said. Then she paused.

"How is he? How is Grandpa?"

Ms. Martha smiled softly. "Oh...I reckon he's ok. He's tired, is all. He's tired and can't get rested. He wants to be out there with Landon, you know. But his body can't keep up at the moment."

Miriam stood quietly. Then she reached over and took Ms. Martha by the hand. "I'm praying for him. I'm praying for Grandpa....and you," she said softly. She couldn't say more because her emotions were taking over so she simply squeezed Ms. Martha's hand before reaching over to grab her sweater and head out the door.

Most days, Miriam received a quick phone call from Abigail, who would use her break at the hospital to check in. Abigail's voice was filled with a new excitement as she spoke about her nurses training. She loved the new job and the people she was meeting. She enjoyed helping both staff and patients and every night she took home books to study. After the supper dishes were washed and put away, Kenny would draw in the writing tablet he had received for his recent birthday and Catherine would fall fast asleep after a bedtime story. When the children were settled, Abigail would take notes from her medical books. One of the nurses had given her a set of blank index cards, and on them she would write out various procedures and protocols. Yes she was tired, she told Miriam. But it was a good tired. And her busy schedule, full of activities and tasks she loved doing, helped assuage any lasting grief from all that had transpired with Matthew.

Ginny Greer had also emerged from her previous shell, relishing in her long-desired role of motherhood. Mrs. Greer practically glowed with a new radiance. Baby Luke was almost 3 months old and was by all accounts a good baby, who only woke up once in the night for a feeding. Mrs. Greer had started coming by the office on Tuesdays and Fridays to bring Luke for a visit. There was never a man so proud as Mr. Greer on those days and no worldly achievements could bring him more fulfillment than he experienced while holding his son in his arms and walking him around to introduce him to the mill workers. On those visiting days, Mr. Greer would take his wife and son uptown for lunch at the cafe. There, all the waitresses would go on and on about how cute baby Luke was and lovely Mrs. Greer was looking. Mrs. Greer always insisted that they bring a sandwich for Miriam when they returned to the mill and Miriam was grateful for it.

WE HAVE THIS HOPE

It was on one of those Tuesdays in March when Mr. Greer walked in the office after lunch and Mrs. Greer was not with him.

"Miriam," Mr. Greer said. "I just ran into Abigail as Ginny and I were leaving the cafe. She was coming to let us know that Philip had driven Ms. Martha and John over from the farm to the hospital because John isn't doing well. He had some kind of episode this morning. Let me take you over to there so you can be with them. Don't worry about anything here at the office. It can wait." His calm demeanor made Miriam calm, despite the fact she was terrified inside. She had known all along that something wasn't right with John.

Abigail was watching out for Miriam and Mr. Greer as they entered the hospital waiting area. She immediately drew Miriam into an embrace.

"It's possible he's had a mild stroke," she said. "But they are taking wonderful care of him right now. And they will be admitting him for a couple nights, to keep a close eye on him."

When Miriam saw Ms. Martha, she couldn't keep the tears from her eyes. Miriam's deep love and gratitude for both John and Ms. Martha was evident in her care for both of them over the coming days. Miriam stayed at the hospital with John and refused to leave, insisting that Ms. Martha go home instead and prepare things for John's return home. Miriam explained to Mr. Greer that she would need to be out of work for a week or two, and he understood. Mrs. Greer agreed to fill in, bringing the baby to the office with her and doing all she could to keep things running smoothly until Miriam could come back.

For the time being, John would be in a wheelchair and would need extra help with the simplest tasks. But Miriam took matters into her own hands, organizing a group of men from the country church to build John a ramp so he could more easily get in the house. She asked Carrie to contact some ladies who might be willing to bring a few meals, until Ms. Martha could get adjusted. Everyone was so kind and willing to do whatever they could to help the Longs, who had served their community faithfully throughout the years.

Next, Miriam talked to Phillip about the farm and what was needed to keep things operational. She knew it was spring planting time and John had been planning out his gardening schedule, as he always did. But this year, even before his episode, he had fallen behind. Phillip was a hard worker but lacked the capacity needed to run things. He took all his instructions from John and it was John who had been trying to help Phillip learn to read. It was John who ordered and supervised and managed the day to day functions of farm life. After taking all of this under consideration, Miriam knew what she needed to do. The Longs needed help. The farm couldn't sustain itself without someone knowledgeable to oversee it.

Miriam waited till Friday evening. She slipped out of the house and drove to the mill, where she quietly entered her office. As she closed the door behind her, she observed from the window the last of the day's light disappear from the horizon. She sat at her desk, took a deep breath, and started to pray.

"Lord, this is all I know to do. I hope it's not a big mistake. I don't even know where to begin or what to say. But like always, I know you'll give me the right words when I need them. Jesus, you are our only hope...so please help me," she said, as she picked up the receiver and started to dial.

CHAPTER TWENTY-SEVEN:

THE ROAD

Miriam's alarm sounded and she quickly rolled over and shut it off. She had hardly slept at all, tossing and turning all through the night hours. Life had certainly been different on the farm since John's stroke. He had been home from the hospital for exactly two weeks and Miriam had yet to return to the mill office. There was just too much to be done for Ms. Martha to handle it all..

As dawn's light began peaking through the curtains, Miriam pulled herself up and quickly made her bed. Once she had dressed, she headed to the kitchen for a quick cup of coffee before going back to help Ms. Martha get John ready for the day. The doctor had told them that, while it may take some months for John to improve from the aftereffects of his stroke, the longterm prognosis was good for him. "He will likely need a cane to walk, and his speech will be a bit altered. He will lack the fine motor skills he had before. But he will adapt over time and so will you," the doctor had told them. But for now, Miriam and Ms. Martha were taking things one day at a time.

For his part, Landon had been very concerned about his grandpa. He had begged to miss a few days of school when John first arrived home from the hospital. Miriam could see how troubled his heart was, so she agreed Landon could stay home for two days. But after that, he needed to get back in class so he wouldn't fall behind.

"Remember what Daddy said about the importance of your studies," she told him.

"I know, Mama. I gotta get my learnin', " Landon affirmed.

After his first day back at school, Landon came running with all his might into the living room, where John was seated in his wheelchair. "Grandpa, Grandpa! I'm home! And guess what, Grandpa? I caught a frog out there at Ol' Tilly's creek bank. Mama wouldn't let me bring it in though. But you'd like it. It's a good 'un. When summer's here, we're gonna go fishin', Grandpa. And you're gonna feel better. And I'm gonna get some good worms for us, so don't you worry."

"Landon, why don't you tell Grandpa what you're studying in school," Miriam said gently.

"I'm learning book stuff, Grandpa. I'm learning about Abraham Lincoln. And he got shot, Grandpa...did you know it? He sure 'nuff did. And he was in a theater and all," he sputtered along, speaking in a flowing stream, with hardly a breath.

"What about math, Landon? Talk about that a minute," Miriam suggested, trying to get him away from the grim thoughts of Lincoln's assassination.

"I'm learnin' my times tables, Grandpa. And I ain't got no use for 'em but Mama says I gotta learn 'em anyway. And Grandma is makin' me learn 'em, too. She says farmers has got to know 'em so they can order supplies and build stuff, like fences and barns and all. Is that true, Grandpa? Did you hafta know times tables?" Landon asked.

Surprisingly, John was able to shake his head slightly and say, "Yeah," with a little chuckle.

"Ok, son. Run on out and do your chores now because the daylight is passing us by," Miriam said.

"Ok, Mama! Bye for now, Grandpa. I gotta do chores. And don't you worry. I'm takin' real good care of the farm," Landon said, as he gave John a big hug before running out the door.

And so it was that one day turned to another and Miriam soon realized it was Tuesday, and the middle of week three since John had come home. She had been praying about a new work schedule, if Mr. Greer would allow it. She was hoping to return to work on Tuesdays and Thursdays for a couple months. Carrie had said she would be glad to come to the farm on the other weekdays and help Ms. Martha with John.

Miriam was also hoping Mr. Greer might consider training one of the Reynolds girls to help in the office. Sarah, the oldest, was very bright. She was quiet and steered clear of gossip and drama. Her temperament was well suited for secretarial work and she would be a great asset, in case the time ever came that Miriam was needed more at home.

As Miriam finished folding the linens, she could hear Ms. Martha working on lunch in the kitchen. Miriam rounded the corner with an arm full of clean dish towels and aprons, when she heard a tentative knock at the back door. Ms. Martha turned to Miriam and asked, "Was that a knock, dear?"

"I believe it was," she answered, as she watched Ms. Martha quickly dry her hands and move towards the door.

As Ms. Martha pulled open the door, Miriam watched as she reached up and clutched her heart. For a moment, Miriam thought Ms. Martha was going to pass out and she ran to steady her.

And there he was. Tall and handsome, Miriam saw him stepping over the threshold to help.

"Mama, Mama....," he said. "Are you okay?"

Ms. Martha was speechless as tears quickly began to stream down her cheeks.

"Merritt...Merritt....my son," she uttered.

"Let's get her to that chair by the table," Miriam said.

After Ms. Martha was seated, Merritt sat across from her on the bench.

"I'm sorry I scared you, Mama. I...I...didn't know the best way...to come back," Merritt spoke. He turned and looked to Miriam.

"You're Miriam then. Nice to meet you face to face" he said, as he stood and shook her hand. Miriam was surprised by him. He wasn't the wild man she had expected. Instead he seemed courteous and well-spoken.

"I didn't know what else to do, Ms. Martha," Miriam spoke up. "I called him and I told him about his dad and about the needs we have here on the farm. I prayed about it and felt it was the right thing to do. And I hope you aren't angry with me. I...I...I didn't know what else to do."

Merritt, sensing Miriam's distress, interjected. "I'm glad she tracked me down and called me, Mama. I've wanted to call you, to see you. But I've made....I've made a mess of things. I failed you, Mama. I failed everyone. I let you and Daddy down. And I know everyone was expecting big things from me and I ended up being such a disappointment. I thought it was best to stay away. For a while I had so much anger. Now I'm just...I'm just ashamed," he said, looking down.

As he was speaking, Miriam's mind wandered back to the conversation she had months ago with Ms. Martha concerning Merritt. He had left for university and soon became captivated by a young sorority student he met there named Jessica. As a debutante from an affluent family, Jessica's upbringing had been much different from Merritt's. But she was enchanted by his striking good looks, his sweet charm, and his career path. Before long, Jessica was introducing Merritt to her friends as, "My future husband, the doctor." Merritt told his parents about Jessica but had never taken her home to meet them. The truth was, Merritt was embarrassed of them and the old farm. Jessica liked modern fashion and big cities and high society living. She introduced Merritt to a whole new culture that included parties and drinking into the wee morning hours. Alcoholic beverages had never been consumed on the farm, so Merritt had no prior experience with them. But once he started carousing, he continued on, refusing to stop. Merritt went from bad to worse when he started spending the night with Jessica, passing out before dawn, and often missing his classes.

It was on his last visit home that Merritt's parents confronted him about his troubling behavior. They begged him to take a semester away from college. "Come on home and get yourself sorted out, son. We will help you," John told him. But Merritt lashed out, "I don't need your help. I'm sick of you both! I'm sick of this farm and the dirt roads and chopping fire wood and pulling corn. I'm leaving and never coming back. Jessica and I have better plans than this disgusting old place," Merritt had shouted, as he slammed the door behind him.

That was the last time that John and Ms. Martha had seen him. It had been four long years and they had no idea what had happened to Merritt but they felt sure it wasn't good. And even though they knew they would never see him again, every morning and night they prayed for him.

When John suffered the stroke, Miriam set about to find Merritt. He deserved to know what was happening to his father. He also needed to help take some responsibility for the farm. It was during a phone call with Merritt's old landlord that Miriam learned the rest of the story. With all the drinking and staying out late, it hadn't been long before Merritt's grades began to drop. Suddenly he had found himself on academic probation, and was eventually expelled. As soon as she realized Merritt was not going to become a doctor, Jessica had left him, and made fun of him in front of their peers. She referred to him as, "the raggedy old farm boy," and, "the dumb redneck." The people he thought were his friends acted like they no longer knew him. When he stopped making his rent payments, the landlord was forced to ask him to vacate his room.

The landlord told Miriam that Merritt had gone to the Salvation Army center for help and he was eventually able to secure a part-time warehouse job, but that was the last he knew of what happened to Merritt.

With this information, Miriam was able to track Merritt's whereabouts and speak to him by phone. She wasn't sure he how would respond to the things she had to say, but she was hopeful he would find his way back home, to the family who still loved him so much.

And now, here he was. Miriam watched as Ms. Martha took out her handkerchief to dry her tears, while Merritt spoke softly.

"Mama, I wanted to ask you and Daddy if I could come back home. I know I don't deserve it but if you could give me a second chance, I will work hard here on the farm. I said things last time that were cruel and unforgivable. You probably don't believe me but I have regretted them many times. I wish I could take it all back but I can't. I want to prove to you that I'm sorry, Mama. I was thinking I could fix up the lean-to on the barn and sleep out there. And I'll do all the spring planting just like Daddy wants it...just like we always did. I know it's getting late in the season and there's so much to be done. But I know farming almost as good as Daddy does and, if we start right now, we have time to get it in the ground. And I will do anything else you need doing around here, Mama. I want you to know....I've given up the way I was living. I don't do those things anymore. So you won't have to worry about that...." Merritt paused. "I guess what I'm saying is I could be like a hired hand, if you'll have me. And if you find it's not working out, you can let me go."

The silence was unbearable until Ms. Martha finally spoke. "Merritt....you aren't a hired hand. You're our son and we love you. We love you so much. And oh how we've missed you. We've missed the sound of your voice...the way you sang while you milked the cows and how you laughed at your daddy's silly stories. We've missed your morning hugs and your clothes in the laundry pile. We've missed seeing you read your Bible on the porch and hearing your prayers at suppertime. Your daddy's had this stroke and he can't speak good right now. But I think it would be best if you talk to him. And I'll come along with you just to make sure he does alright because it's going to be a shock for him to see you, son. It's a shock for me. But it's an answer to lots of prayers. I'd 'bout given up. Many days I didn't feel like praying because I was tired and weary. But to see you here, son...to hold your hand and hear your voice right here at the table again....that's a miracle. I've been hoping and now hope is here."

Hearing those words, Merritt slipped down on his knees in front of his mother, placed his head on her lap, and cried. "Please forgive me, Mama. I love you, Mama, and I'm so sorry for the bad I've done"

Miriam couldn't help but cry herself because repentance is a beautiful thing. After a few quiet moments, Ms. Martha and Merritt went into the living room to find John. Miriam wanted to follow behind them but realized that would be an intrusion. Those moments were for them....for two parents and their prodigal son, who was returning home.

Miriam tidied the kitchen and stirred a big pot of pinto beans which were being prepared for supper. After half an hour, Merritt walked back to the kitchen, looking weary yet relieved. "Want some coffee," Miriam asked him.

"Oh yes, ma'am. That would be really nice," he answered.

"The weather is so pretty. Sometimes I like to stand on the porch and take in the sunshine," she told him.

"I'd like that a lot," he said.

They stood side by side, looking out on the farm. There was a gentle breeze in the air and Miriam felt at peace.

"These are the fields of my boyhood," Merritt spoke. "Where I romped and played and caught lightning bugs and built snowmen. I asked Jesus in my heart down there by the windmill. I remember it like it was yesterday even though that seems so long ago now. Daddy had me get on my knees and say the sinner's prayer. I took it all for granted, Miriam. I never realized how blessed I was. And to have the love of my parents and a community all around me. Nothing this world offers comes close to that. I wonder if the people will accept me back?"

"Of course they will," Miriam responded. "You're one of their own and they love you. I think the thing you'll have to do, Merritt, is learn to forgive yourself. We all make mistakes. But we can't live back there in them. Once the good Lord forgives us, we have to move forward and live in the here and now. My husband had a saying he used to tell me quite a bit. He said that life is for the living."

"Sounds like he was a smart man," Merritt said.

"Oh yes. He was smart...and kind. He would like you and he would be your friend," Miriam said, with a soft smile.

Merritt pointed to the old fence. "See that road over there? I've walked that dirt road a million times. I remember the last time I walked it out of here. I thought I would never see it again. But today, that road never looked so good. That's the road that brought me home."

"That road didn't bring you home, Merritt, " Miriam whispered tenderly, as she caught sight of a bluebird, flying towards its nest. "God did. God brought you home...at last."

WE HAVE THIS HOPE

Printed in Great Britain
by Amazon